SHADOWS OF A
WITCH
BLAKE PATRICK

Copywrite

For more information:

To sign up for my free newsletter please visit website: Https://blake-patrick.co.uk[1]

Email: info@blake-patrick.co.uk

---

1. https://blake-patrick.co.uk

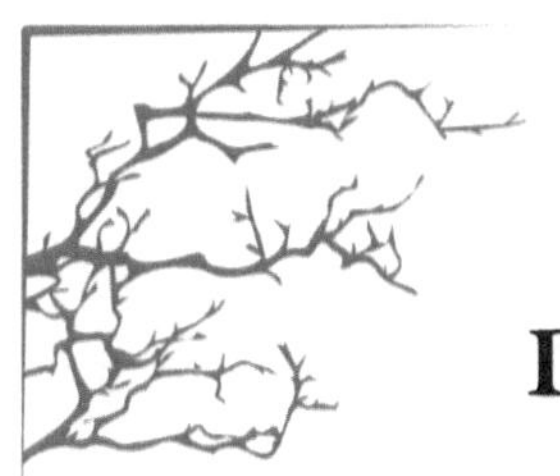

DEDICATION

To my beloved wife, Carrie,

For over 40 years, you have been my muse, my unwavering source of inspiration, and my guiding light through the darkest of creative journeys. This book, "Shadow of a witch" is a testament to your unwavering support and belief in my storytelling.

Your encouragement, patience, and love have fuelled my imagination and given life to the characters and worlds within these pages. It is your strength that echoes in the resilience of the heroes and heroines who face the malevolent forces of Ravenwood Manor.

As we embark on yet another chapter of our own adventure, I dedicate this book to you, my rock, my partner, and my love. Your unwavering presence in my life is a story of love and inspiration that transcends the pages of any novel.

With all my love
Blake

LITTLE BOY LOST

"Where on earth is Father Thomas?" Sister Edith exclaimed as she walked briskly down the corridor of the orphanage. "It feels like I've been looking for him forever!"

in a frustrated tone. Her black habit flowing like a dark troubling river behind her as she quickened her pace.

She heard a noise at the end of the corridor and almost felt relieved to have eventually found him. As she reached the door the corridor was silent once more. She reached for the handle and pushing it slowly open she gasped as she took in the scene before her.

Father Thomas was nailed to the wall in a crucifix position and obviously dead, blood slowly seeping from deep wounds across his forehead, his eyes staring lifelessly directly at her. Sister Edith screamed, turning around immediately and started running back down the corridor. She ran to the office and picked up the phone dialling 999, the phone shaking in her hand.

"Which emergency service do you require?" the automated voice came through the handset.

"Um, ambulance, no police, I don't know, just someone". The call rang through to the ambulance service.

"Ambulance service, is the patient breathing?",

"No, he's been nailed to a wall!" Sister Edith wailed.

In what seemed like an eternity, Sister Edith felt relieved on seeing the blue flashing lights of the Emergency services on route to her. The ambulance screeched to a halt outside the massive front doors of the Orphanage, with the lights still flashing now illuminating the children's faces in the first-floor windows, who had been awoken by the loud sirens.

"Where is the patient?" a young-looking paramedic shouted to Sister Edith. "I'll show you" she replied. They both ran down the corridor to the bizarre scene.

"Bloody hell" the astonished paramedic blurted out. He had not seen anything like this before in his fairly short two-year career. He ran to Father Thomas, grabbing a chair as he raced across the floor. He clambered up on the chair and immediately felt for a pulse, nothing.

He slowly climbed off the chair staring up at the Priest's body, his legs wobbling a bit from the shock. He pulled at his shoulder mike, "2 Alpha, the patient is deceased, can you call the police, better have CID". He turned to see Sister Edith on her knees, sobbing into her hands.

20 minutes later, Ds Karl Cushnahan arrived at the scene.

A young bobby was standing at the front doors holding a clipboard.

"Who else is here, John?" "Just me and Jack Warner, who is taping the corridor off, the Sister and a bunch of kids upstairs. The DS strode up the steps in turned right into the long corridor, where he saw Pc Jack Warner tying police crime scene tape across from one side to the other to prevent any unauthorised access.

"Jack, what have we got? ".

"Dead body of the Priest in the room at the far end, weirdest thing I ever saw Sarge, I can guarantee you've never had one of these before!"

Ds Cushnahan walked down the corridor and pushed the door open with his toes. "Jesus" he exclaimed. It was like a scene out of some horror movie. He turned back and walked back to where Pc Warner waited.

"Told yer" said Jack.

"Where's the Sister?" he asked Jack.

"In the office just past the entry doors". He walked to the office and on entering was faced with a red eyed nun.

"I'm sorry for your loss" was all he could muster. "What happened?" he asked, "I was looking for Father Thomas for about half an hour but couldn't find him. I then heard a noise from the room at the end of the corridor and that's where I found him."

"Did he say anything?",

"No, he was already dead, who would do such a thing?"

"I've no idea but I plan to find out. We will need a statement from you, if that's okay?"

"Of course, officer".

Of all the children staring out in wonder at the scene outside, one had a slight smirk on his face.

DS Karl Cushnahan paced around the crime scene, his thoughts racing as he tried to make sense of the gruesome tableau before him. The room seemed to radiate an eerie chill, and the crucifixion-style murder of Father Thomas was unlike anything he had encountered in his years on the force.

Chris Corbett, a CSI officer was busy snapping pictures of the crime scene. Every click of the camera felt like a gunshot in the oppressive silence of the corridor.

"Chris, make sure you capture every angle," Karl instructed, his voice low and steady. "We need to document every detail, no matter how macabre."

As they continued their grim task, Karl couldn't shake the feeling that this case was going to be unlike any other. The manner of Father Thomas's death was not only horrifying but also deeply symbolic. It hinted at a darkness that reached far beyond the walls of the orphanage.

Turning to Sister Edith, Karl approached her gently. Her eyes were swollen from crying, and her hands trembled as she clutched her rosary beads.

"Sister Edith," he began, "I know this is a difficult time for you, but we need your cooperation to understand what happened here. Can you think of anyone who might have had a grudge against Father Thomas?"

The nun shook her head, her voice quivering.

"Father Thomas was a kind man. He never harmed anyone. I can't imagine who would do such a terrible thing."

Karl nodded sympathetically.

"We'll do everything we can to find out who did this, Sister. In the meantime, we'll need you to provide a formal statement to our officers. It will help us piece together the events leading up to this."

As Sister Edith composed herself to give her statement, Karl couldn't help but notice the children upstairs, their faces filled with a mix of fear and curiosity. Among them, one child stood out, staring at the policemen intently. Karl made a mental note to speak with that child later; something about his expression didn't sit right.

The investigation into Father Thomas's gruesome murder took an unsettling turn as DS Karl Cushnahan delved deeper into the case. He spent hours interviewing the staff and children at the orphanage, searching for any leads that might shed light on the motive behind the horrifying crime.

The children's stories varied, but one thing was clear: none of them had witnessed the murder or knew who could have committed such an act. As Karl questioned them, he couldn't help but feel a growing unease about the whole situation. It was as though the orphanage held dark secrets that were buried deep beneath its walls.

The child from earlier, named Samuel, caught Karl's attention once again. He decided it was time to speak with the boy in private, away from the prying eyes of the other children.

"Come with me, Sam," Karl said, gesturing for the boy to follow him down the quiet corridor. They entered an empty room, and Karl closed the door behind them.

"Now, Sam," Karl began, crouching down to the boy's eye level, "I couldn't help but notice that you had a peculiar expression on your face when we found Father Thomas. Do you know anything about what happened?"

Sam hesitated for a moment, his gaze shifting to the floor.

Then, in a small voice, he replied, "I saw something, but I don't know if it's important."

Karl leaned in closer, his voice gentle. "Sam, every detail matters in a case like this. Please, tell me what you saw."

The boy took a deep breath and finally spoke. "I saw a shadowy figure, like a woman, standing by Father Thomas's body. She had long, dark hair and a black cloak. She looked at me, and her eyes...they glowed red." If he was honest, Sam didn't really know what happened, one minute Father Thomas was shouting at him, for what he couldn't quite remember, and the next Father Thomas was on the wall. But he wasn't sad about it, he was rather pleased. Father Thomas had made his life hell in the past couple of months, so good riddance.

Karl's heart raced as he listened to Sam's description. A shadowy figure with glowing red eyes? It was as though the orphanage's dark secrets were beginning to unravel, and the horror of what they would discover sent shivers down his spine.

The chilling revelation from young Samuel about the shadowy figure with glowing red eyes sent shivers down DS Karl Cushnahan's spine. It was a detail that added a layer of the supernatural to an already horrifying murder.

Karl decided to dig deeper into the history of the orphanage. He needed to uncover any hidden secrets that might provide a clue to the identity of the mysterious figure Samuel had described.

Sister Edith, still shaken from the traumatic discovery, sat in the office with Karl as they went through old records and documents.

"Sister," Karl began, "have there been any unusual occurrences or legends associated with this place? Anything that might explain what Samuel saw?"

Sister Edith hesitated before responding, "There have been rumours, stories passed down through generations of nuns who have served here. They speak of a witch, an evil presence that haunts the orphanage. But I never believed such tales."

Karl furrowed his brow.

"A witch? It seems far-fetched, but we can't dismiss anything at this point. Do you have any records or writings about this supposed witch?"

Sister Edith nodded and retrieved an old journal from a dusty shelf. It belonged to a nun who had served at the orphanage decades ago. As Karl flipped through the pages, he found entries detailing strange occurrences, unexplained deaths, and sightings of a shadowy woman with glowing red eyes.

"This is disturbing," Karl muttered. "It appears that there's more to this place than meets the eye. We need to find out if there's any truth to these stories."

As night fell and the orphanage seemed to grow darker,

Karl and his team continued their investigation. They couldn't ignore the possibility that a centuries-old curse or black force was at play, and it was up to them to unravel the truth before more lives were claimed by the shadow of the witch.

DS Karl Cushnahan delved deeper into the chilling history of the orphanage, uncovering more disturbing accounts of the shadowy figure with glowing red eyes. The pieces of the puzzle were slowly coming together, revealing a connection between the past and the horrifying murder of Father Thomas.

Karl summoned Sister Edith once more, her eyes heavy with exhaustion. "Sister, these journal entries suggest a pattern of unexplained deaths and sightings of the shadowy woman. Can you think of anyone who might have more information about this? Perhaps an older nun who has been here for a long time?"

Sister Edith nodded slowly.

"There is one nun, Sister Agnes, who has been with the orphanage for decades. She might know more about the history and the stories surrounding the witch."

Karl wasted no time. He and Sister Edith sought out Sister Agnes, a frail and elderly nun who had witnessed decades of history within the orphanage's walls. Their journey led them to Ravenswood Manor, home of the Carrington family, a large estate comprising of a large manor house with several annexes.

In one of those annexes Sister Agnes sat in a dimly lit room, a sense of foreboding hanging heavy in the air.

"Sister Agnes," Karl began, "we need your help. We've discovered journal entries that speak of a witch and strange occurrences here. Can you shed some light on these stories?"

Sister Agnes's trembling hands reached for Karl's outstretched hand, her eyes clouded with a mixture of fear and uncertainty. She knew that the secrets of Ravenwood Manor ran deep, and the journal entries he spoke of hinted at a darkness that had long been shrouded in mystery.

Taking a deep breath to steady herself, Sister Agnes nodded slowly.

"I can tell you what I know," she replied, her voice quivering.

"But you must promise me that you will be careful, for there are things within these walls that should never be awakened."

Karl exchanged a glance with his fellow officers, recognising the gravity of the situation. "We promise, Sister Agnes," he assured her. "We're here to uncover the truth and bring justice to those who may have been wronged."

With a sense of resolve, Sister Agnes led the detectives through the dimly lit corridors of Ravenwood Manor, her footsteps echoing in the silence. The walls seemed to hold their secrets close, the very air imbued with an unsettling presence.

As they reached the heart of the manor, Sister Agnes entered a small, candlelit room filled with ancient tomes and artifacts. It was a room that had been off-limits to most, a place where the history of the Carrington family was meticulously documented.

Sister Agnes's trembling hands reached for a weathered leather-bound journal, its pages yellowed with age. She carefully opened it and began to read aloud, her voice filled with a sense of foreboding.

"In the year 1692, a darkness descended upon Ravenwood Manor," she began, her eyes scanning the faded ink. "The Carrington family was said to possess a power—an ancient magic that had been passed down through the generations. But with that power came a curse, a malevolence that could not be contained."

Karl and his fellow detectives listened intently as Sister Agnes continued to recount the history of the Carrington family. She spoke of rituals, incantations, and a sorcerer who had sought to harness the family's magic for his own dark purposes.

"Legend has it that the sorcerer's power grew so great that he could manipulate reality itself," Sister Agnes whispered, her voice barely above a breath. "He used his dark magic to commit unspeakable acts, and Ravenwood Manor became a place of fear and despair."

As the words hung in the air, a chill settled over the room, and the flickering candle flames cast eerie shadows on the walls. Karl couldn't help but feel that they were on the cusp of a revelation— a revelation that would unearth the truth behind Father Thomas's murder and the forces that had long haunted Ravenwood Manor.

Sister Agnes's trembling hands closed the journal, its secrets once again hidden from view.

"There is much more to the story," she said, her gaze fixed on the detectives, "but I fear that the darkness that once plagued this place may still linger. You must be cautious in your pursuit of the truth, for some secrets are best left undisturbed."

Karl nodded solemnly, his determination unwavering.

"We will uncover the truth, Sister Agnes," he vowed, "and put an end to the evil that has plagued Ravenwood Manor for far too long."

With those words, the detectives and Sister Edith left the candlelit room, their path set on a treacherous journey into the heart of darkness. The secrets of the Carrington family and the sorcerer's legacy awaited, and they would stop at nothing to uncover the truth, no matter how perilous the path ahead.

In the following years, Ds Karl Cushnahan's pursuit of the truth led him down countless winding paths and through numerous dead ends. The mysteries of Ravenwood Manor and the forces that had plagued it remained elusive, like shadows that slipped through his grasp.

Despite his unwavering determination and tireless efforts, the detective found himself facing insurmountable challenges. The secrets hidden within the walls of the manor were guarded by a power beyond his comprehension, and the darkness that had once consumed Samuel Carrington had receded into obscurity.

As time passed, Ds Cushnahan grew frustrated and disheartened. The case of Father Thomas's murder continued to haunt him, a relentless reminder of the unsolved mystery that had driven him to Ravenwood Manor in the first place.

But Ds Cushnahan was not one to give up easily. He vowed to find the priest's killer, to bring closure to the case that had consumed his thoughts and his career. He poured over old case files, revisited witnesses, and chased down leads, determined to uncover the truth no matter how long it took.

Years turned into decades, and Ds Cushnahan aged, but his resolve remained unyielding. He became a legend in the world of detective work, known for his relentless pursuit of justice.

The case of Father Thomas's murder became his life's work, a mission that he would never abandon. And so, the detective continued his quest, vowing to find the priest's killer and to unearth the secrets of Ravenwood Manor. The darkness that had eluded him for so long would not remain hidden forever, and Ds Karl Cushnahan was determined to bring it into the light, no matter the cost.

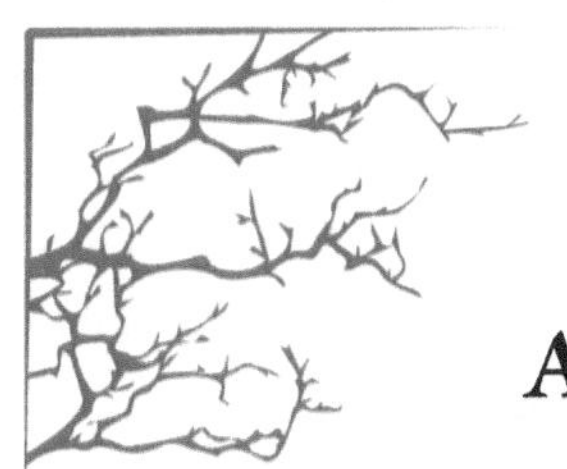

A NEW HOME

The grand English countryside estate of the Carrington family was a sprawling marvel of old-world opulence. Nestled amidst rolling hills and lush greenery, it stood as a testament to the wealth and prestige of the Carrington's, one of the most affluent families in the country. The estate, known as Ravenwood Manor, was a magnificent mansion that had been in the Carrington family for generations.

Sir Robert Carrington, the patriarch of the family, was a distinguished gentleman with silver hair and an air of authority that commanded respect. He was the CEO of Carrington Industries, a colossal conglomerate with interests spanning finance, technology, and manufacturing. A man of power and influence, Sir Robert was known for his charitable endeavours and his commitment to preserving the family legacy.

One sunny morning, Sir Robert and his wife, Lady Eleanor Carrington, stood at the front of Ravenwood Manor, their eyes filled with anticipation. They were about to welcome a new member into their family, a young, orphaned boy named Samuel.

Samuel, a ten-year-old with raven-black hair and striking emerald eyes, had spent most of his life in the large orphanage on the outskirts of London, scene of the grisly murder of a priest year earlier. His parents had died in a tragic accident when he was just a baby, leaving him with no memory of them.

For years, he had dreamt of a better life, and that dream was about to become a reality. The Carrington's had chosen Samuel to be their adopted son after hearing about his exceptional intelligence and promising potential. Lady Eleanor had always longed for a child, and when she had seen Samuel's photograph, something deep within her had told her that he was meant to be part of their family.

As Samuel stepped out of the chauffeured car and gazed upon Ravenwood Manor, his heart swelled with a mixture of excitement and trepidation. The estate was unlike anything he had ever seen, a magnificent palace that seemed like something out of a fairy tale.

Sir Robert extended a welcoming hand to Samuel, his face adorned with a warm smile.

"Welcome to Ravenwood Manor, Samuel," he said with a kind tone. "We're delighted to have you join our family."

Samuel, overwhelmed by the grandeur of his new surroundings, managed a shy smile.

"Thank you, Sir Robert," he replied softly.

Lady Eleanor, elegant in her demeanour, knelt down to Samuel's eye level and embraced him.

"You may call me Lady Eleanor, my dear," she said warmly. "We hope you'll come to think of this place as your home."

Touched by their kindness, Samuel nodded. He had never imagined he would find himself in such a luxurious setting, surrounded by people who genuinely cared about him. His heart swelled with gratitude.

Inside Ravenwood Manor, Samuel was introduced to the household staff, each person greeting him with warm smiles and words of welcome. He met Mrs Jenkins, the kind-hearted housekeeper, and James, the jovial cook who promised to prepare all of Samuel's favourite dishes.

As Samuel settled into his new room, he couldn't help but feel a sense of wonder. The room was spacious and beautifully adorned with antique furniture and plush carpets. He had never owned so many toys and books before, and he couldn't wait to explore them all.

In the days that followed, Samuel's life at Ravenwood Manor was a whirlwind of excitement and new experiences. He spent his mornings studying with a private tutor, immersing himself in subjects ranging from mathematics to literature. Lady Eleanor had a passion for art, and she introduced Samuel to the world of painting, encouraging him to express his creativity.

Afternoons were filled with adventures around the vast estate. Samuel roamed the manicured gardens, explored the hidden corners of the mansion, and even had picnics by the tranquil lake on the property. The Carrington's treated him with a love and care he had never known, and Samuel blossomed under their guidance.

Sir Robert, a shrewd businessman, often took Samuel to his office and explained the intricacies of the family's vast empire. Samuel was fascinated by the world of finance and technology, and he absorbed every piece of information with an insatiable hunger for knowledge.

However, amidst the idyllic days, there were moments when Samuel felt a strange unease. He would sometimes hear whispered voices in the corridors, fleeting shadows that seemed to disappear when he turned to look. These odd occurrences were unsettling, but Samuel dismissed them as mere figments of his imagination.

One evening, as Samuel was reading in the library, he overheard a hushed conversation between Sir Robert and Lady Eleanor in the adjacent room. Intrigued, he couldn't resist eavesdropping.

"They must never know, Eleanor," Sir Robert's voice was tinged with urgency. "The power he possesses...it's beyond anything we've ever seen."

Lady Eleanor's voice was equally anxious. "But Robert, he's just a child. He doesn't understand the extent of his abilities."

Samuel's heart raced as he listened to their conversation. What were they talking about? What power did he possess? He had always felt different, but he had never understood why.

As days turned into weeks, the strange occurrences at Ravenwood Manor escalated. Samuel's unease grew as he witnessed objects moving on their own and heard disembodied whispers that seemed to call his name.

One night, as he lay in his bed, Samuel felt a presence in his room. The air grew cold, and he saw a shadowy figure with glowing red eyes standing at the foot of his bed. Terror gripped him, and he tried to scream, but no sound escaped his lips.

The figure spoke in a chilling, otherworldly voice.

"You have the power, Samuel. Embrace it, and you will be unstoppable."

Samuel's heart pounded as he realised that he was not alone in his room. The shadowy presence seemed to feed on his fear, growing stronger with each passing moment.

In the darkness of his room, Samuel mustered all the courage he could find. With a trembling voice, he asked, "Who are you? What do you want from me?"

The shadowy figure chuckled, a sound that sent shivers down Samuel's spine.

"I am the embodiment of your true self, Samuel. You have a gift, a power that can reshape the world to your will. But you must let go of your fear and embrace the darkness within."

Samuel's mind raced as he grappled with the words of the shadowy presence. What did it mean to embrace the darkness within? And what was this power it spoke of?

Before he could gather his thoughts, the figure vanished, leaving Samuel in the cold darkness of his room. The events of that night haunted his dreams, and he awoke the next morning with a sense of dread that clung to him like a shadow.

Samuel couldn't shake off the feeling that something sinister was lurking within him. He confided in Mrs. Jenkins, the housekeeper, about the strange events he had witnessed. She listened with a concerned expression and promised to speak to Sir Robert and Lady Eleanor about it.

As the days passed, Samuel's unease grew, and he became increasingly withdrawn. The once-bustling mansion felt like a maze of secrets, and he had no one he could trust.

In the quiet countryside, where the whisper of the wind through the trees was the only sound to break the stillness, Samuel Carrington grew up in the imposing shadow of Ravenwood Manor. From a young age, there was something unsettling about him, a darkness that seemed to linger in his gaze and the curl of his lips.

As a child, Samuel revelled in the twisted delights of his secluded surroundings. He would wander the grounds of the estate, his footsteps echoing against the ancient cobblestones as he sought out the creatures that called Ravenwood Manor home. In the depths of the forest, he would find unsuspecting animals, their innocent eyes meeting his with a silent plea for mercy.

The rustle of leaves underfoot, the distant call of nocturnal creatures, and the chill of the night air—all of these sensations fuelled Samuel's malevolent desires. His fingers would twitch with anticipation as he approached his unsuspecting victims, a wicked grin spreading across his face at the thought of the torment to come.

With a wicked grin, Samuel would unleash his cruelty upon the helpless creatures, revelling in their pain and suffering. He took pleasure in their screams, in the twisted dance of malevolence that played out in the shadows of Ravenwood Manor.

His laughter echoed through the forest, a chilling symphony of darkness that sent shivers down the spines of all who heard it. But Samuel was deaf to their cries, consumed by the exhilaration of his own wickedness.

As the moon cast its pale glow over the land, Samuel's silhouette would dance against the walls of Ravenwood Manor, a sinister figure cloaked in darkness. He was the master of his domain, the puppeteer of a macabre spectacle that played out in the depths of the night.

One fateful night, as Samuel prowled the grounds of Ravenwood Manor, a strange sensation washed over him. It was as if the very air around him crackled with an unseen energy, beckoning him deeper into the heart of darkness.

In the moonlit courtyard, Samuel felt a surge of power coursing through his veins, awakening something primal and ancient within him. He reached out with trembling hands, his fingertips brushing against the cool stone of the manor's walls.

And then it happened—a spark of malevolent energy surged from his fingertips, illuminating the night with an eerie glow. Samuel's eyes widened in disbelief as he realised the true extent of his power.

One evening, while wandering the dimly lit hallways, Samuel stumbled upon a hidden door. It led to a dusty, forgotten chamber filled with ancient books and artifacts. Among them was a tome bound in dark leather, its pages filled with cryptic symbols and incantations.

Samuel's curiosity got the better of him, and he began to decipher the contents of the mysterious tome. It was a grimoire, a book of spells and rituals that promised unimaginable power to its wielder. The more he read, the more he felt a dark energy coursing through him.

As Samuel delved deeper into the forbidden knowledge, his innocence began to wane, replaced by an insidious hunger for power. He practiced the incantations in secret, his abilities growing stronger with each passing day.

With newfound excitement coursing through his veins, Samuel delved deeper into the forbidden secrets of the dark arts. He spent hours poring over ancient tomes and grimoires, his mind hungry for the knowledge that would unlock his true potential.

In the depths of Ravenwood Manor's library, Samuel practiced the incantations and rituals that would shape his destiny. He spoke words of power that reverberated through the air, weaving a web of darkness that ensnared all who dared to cross his path.

As the flickering candlelight cast eerie shadows across the pages of the ancient texts, Samuel's eyes gleamed with a fervour bordering on madness. He was consumed by a thirst for power, a hunger that could never be sated.

Under the cover of night, Samuel would venture into the depths of the forest, where the veil between worlds grew thin. There, he would commune with dark entities that whispered secrets of untold power in his ears.

With each passing day, Samuel's mastery of the dark arts grew stronger, his malevolent influence spreading like a cancer throughout the land. He revelled in his newfound abilities, using them to sow chaos and despair wherever he went.

As the moon hung low in the sky, Samuel would conduct his sinister rituals beneath its watchful gaze, his chants echoing through the darkness like a twisted hymn to the forces of evil. He was a malevolent force to be reckoned with, a harbinger of darkness in a world blinded by its own ignorance.

As Samuel Carrington's power reached its zenith, he became a malevolent force to be reckoned with. His name struck fear into the hearts of all who heard it, and his presence cast a shadow over the land.

But little did the world know that Samuel's reign of darkness was only just beginning. With his twisted powers at his command, he would stop at nothing to bend the world to his will, plunging it into an era of darkness and despair unlike any other. And in the heart of Ravenwood Manor, the true malevolence of Samuel Carrington would be unleashed upon the world.

Unbeknownst to the Carrington's, the boy they had welcomed into their home was no longer the innocent child they had adopted. Samuel had become something else, something dark and sinister, driven by a thirst for power that would stop at nothing to achieve its goals.

Little did Sir Robert and Lady Eleanor know that their decision to adopt Samuel had set in motion a chain of events that would plunge their family into a nightmare beyond their wildest imagination. The darkness that had taken hold of Samuel was about to consume them all, and Ravenwood Manor would become a place of unspeakable horrors.

LIFE OF LUXURY

Months passed since Samuel's unsettling discovery of the hidden grimoire, and Ravenwood Manor had settled into a facade of normalcy. The grandeur of the estate and the luxurious lifestyle provided by the Carrington's had become Samuel's new reality. The once-quiet orphan now revelled in a life of opulence that he could scarcely have imagined.

Sir Robert and Lady Eleanor, proud of Samuel's quick wit and his thirst for knowledge, continued to nurture his talents. They believed their adoptive son was thriving in his new environment, unaware of the dark path he was secretly treading.

Samuel had grown more proficient in his studies, his intellect surpassing that of his peers. However, his newfound power, fuelled by the grimoire's forbidden knowledge, had become a dangerous secret he could no longer contain.

One evening, as Samuel was alone in his room, he decided to experiment with a spell he had been practicing in secret.

The incantations Samuel spoke were ancient words of power, passed down through generations of dark practitioners of the occult. They were words imbued with malevolent energy, designed to bend the very fabric of reality to the will of the one who spoke them.

As Samuel stood in the dim candlelight of his chamber, the words spilled from his lips like a sinister melody, each syllable carrying the weight of centuries of arcane knowledge. The air around him seemed to crackle with a palpable energy, and the very walls of his room seemed to pulsate with dark intent.

With each word spoken, the incantation wove its tendrils into the fabric of the universe, bending it to Samuel's will. Objects within his chamber responded to the call of his power, defying gravity and floating gently in the air as if guided by unseen hands.

To Samuel's amazement, the incantation he had spoken had unlocked a power within him that he had only dared to dream of. He watched in awe as the objects in his room danced in the air, their movements a testament to the dark forces at his command.

But even as he revelled in his newfound abilities, a sense of foreboding crept over him. He knew that with great power came great responsibility, and that the path he had chosen would lead him down a dark and dangerous road. Yet, he was undeterred, for the allure of power and the promise of mastery over the forces of darkness were too great to resist.

Samuel grinned with satisfaction, revelling in the sense of power coursing through him. He had kept his abilities hidden, but now he felt the urge to test the limits of his new found magic. As he honed his skills, he became increasingly aware of the extent of his potential to shape reality to his will.

However, Samuel also felt a growing darkness within him, an insatiable hunger for more power. The grimoire's promises of limitless abilities had taken hold of him, and he couldn't resist its allure.

As Samuel's abilities grew, so did his arrogance. He began to manipulate his surroundings, subtly altering events to his advantage. In school, he excelled effortlessly, his mind absorbing knowledge like a sponge. He used his magic to influence his classmates and teachers, ensuring that he always came out on top.

Outside the walls of Ravenwood Manor, Samuel's influence extended into the business world. He would accompany Sir Robert to meetings and negotiations, using his powers to sway decisions in the family's favour. Carrington Industries thrived under Samuel's secret guidance, and the family's wealth continued to soar to new heights.

But there was a cost to Samuel's actions. The more he delved into the dark arts, the more detached he became from his humanity. He could no longer feel empathy or remorse, and the sense of right and wrong had blurred into obscurity.

As Samuel's powers continued to grow, he began to notice an alarming change in Ravenwood Manor itself. The mansion seemed to react to his presence, its walls echoing with whispers that only he could hear. Shadows danced in the corners of his vision, and the once-majestic estate began to take on an eerie, foreboding aura.

Lady Eleanor had sensed the shift in Samuel's demeanour. She noticed the way his eyes had changed, their once-innocent sparkle now replaced by a chilling, calculating gaze. She confided in Sir Robert about her concerns, fearing that their adopted son was slipping away from them.

Sir Robert, always pragmatic, dismissed her worries.

"He's a gifted child, Eleanor," he reassured her. "It's natural for him to be a bit eccentric. Besides, he's the future of Carrington Industries. We need him to be exceptional."

But Lady Eleanor couldn't shake off her unease. She couldn't help but feel that something dark and insidious was taking hold of Samuel, and she was determined to uncover the truth. One evening, Lady Eleanor decided to confront Samuel about her suspicions. She found him in his room, surrounded by flickering candles and an air of secrecy.

"Samuel," she began gently, "there's something I need to discuss with you. You've been acting differently lately, and I'm worried about you."

Samuel, aware that his secret was at risk, masked his emotions with practiced ease.

"What do you mean, Mother?" he asked innocently.

Lady Eleanor sighed; her concern etched on her face.

"I've seen the changes in you, Samuel. Your powers, your demeanour— it's as though you're becoming someone else. I fear that you're losing yourself in this pursuit of knowledge and power."

Samuel feigned surprise. "Mother, you worry too much. I'm just trying to live up to the expectations you and Father have for me."

Lady Eleanor wasn't convinced. She had known Samuel since he was a child, and the boy she had once loved and nurtured seemed to be slipping away. She was determined to uncover the truth, no matter the cost.

Despite Lady Eleanor's concerns, Samuel continued to delve deeper into the dark arts. He would spend hours in the hidden chamber, poring over the grimoire's pages, and practicing spells that defied the laws of nature.

One evening, as the moon hung low in the sky, Samuel attempted a spell that would grant him the ability to see into the future. He chanted the incantation with a fervour that bordered on obsession. As he closed his eyes and focused his energy, he felt a surge of power unlike anything he had experienced before.

Images flashed before his mind's eye—visions of wealth, power, and dominion. Samuel saw himself at the helm of Carrington Industries, his control absolute, his rivals crushed beneath his heel. He would become the most influential man in the world, reshaping reality to suit his desires.

But in the midst of these visions, Samuel also glimpsed a darker, more malevolent future. He saw himself as a tyrant, ruling with an iron fist, his heart consumed by greed and cruelty.

It was a future he had once feared but was now embracing with open arms. Samuel's newfound abilities began to take a toll on his physical and mental well-being. He would often wake in the dead of night, drenched in cold sweat, haunted by nightmares of the darkness that had enveloped him. The once-bright eyes that had captured Lady Eleanor's heart were now dull and lifeless.

Lady Eleanor, undeterred by Samuel's attempts to conceal his secret, sought the guidance of experts in the occult. She reached out to scholars and mystics who could shed light on the dark path her adopted son had embarked upon.

One evening, as the clock struck midnight, a renowned psychic arrived at Ravenwood Manor. Lady Eleanor had arranged a private session in the hopes of uncovering the truth about Samuel's transformation.

The psychic, a woman with piercing blue eyes and an air of mystery, entered Samuel's room, her presence filling the space with an otherworldly energy. She closed her eyes and began to chant incantations, her hands hovering over Samuel's head.

As the psychic delved into Samuel's consciousness, she encountered a dark and turbulent sea of emotions. She saw glimpses of his growing power, his insatiable hunger for control, and the force that had taken hold of him.

With a gasp, the psychic withdrew, her face pale with dread.

"There is a darkness within him," she whispered to Lady Eleanor. "A force beyond our comprehension. It is consuming him, and it seeks to unleash chaos upon the world."

Lady Eleanor's heart sank at the revelation. She knew that the situation was far graver than she had imagined. The fate of her family and the world itself now hung in the balance, and she was determined to confront Samuel and save him from the abyss of his own making.

Unbeknownst to Samuel, the forces of light and darkness were converging upon Ravenwood Manor. The Carrington family stood at the precipice of a battle that would determine the destiny of their adopted son and the world itself.

THE UNEXPLAINED INCIDENTS

As the days grew colder and the shadows lengthened at Ravenwood Manor, the atmosphere within its hallowed halls became increasingly tense. Lady Eleanor had discovered the truth about Samuel's descent into darkness, and she knew that she had to act swiftly to save her adopted son from the forces that gripped him.

One evening, she gathered Sir Robert and a select group of trusted individuals in the drawing room. Among them were Dr Margaret Stirling, a renowned psychologist, and Professor Edward Sinclair, an expert in the occult.

"Thank you all for coming," Lady Eleanor began with a solemn tone. "We are facing a grave situation, one that threatens not only our family but also the world itself. Samuel has become a vessel for a dark and insidious power, and we must find a way to free him from its clutches."

Sir Robert nodded gravely; his concern etched on his face.

"I will do whatever it takes to save our son," he declared.

Dr Stirling, her brow furrowed in deep thought, spoke next.

"We must first understand the extent of Samuel's condition. I propose a series of psychological assessments and consultations to determine the nature of the darkness within him."

In the following weeks, Samuel found himself thrust into a whirlwind of psychological assessments, each session conducted under the watchful eye of Dr Stirling, a renowned psychiatrist known for his expertise in unravelling the complexities of the human mind.

The sessions took place in a dimly lit room within the confines of Ravenwood Manor, where the walls seemed to whisper secrets of the past and the shadows danced with unseen entities. Samuel sat across from Dr Stirling, the air heavy with tension as they delved into the depths of his troubled psyche.

Dr Stirling's probing questions cut through the silence like a knife, each one designed to peel back the layers of Samuel's consciousness and expose the dark secrets hidden within. Samuel felt as though he were being dissected, his innermost thoughts laid bare for scrutiny.

As the sessions progressed, Dr Stirling led Samuel down a labyrinthine path of introspection, guiding him through memories both painful and profound. They explored the twisted corridors of his mind, where shadows lurked in every corner and echoes of past traumas reverberated through the darkness.

With each session, Samuel found himself confronting demons he had long buried, memories of his childhood cruelty and the sinister urges that had plagued him since youth. Dr Stirling's calm demeanour served as a beacon of stability in the tumultuous storm of Samuel's mind, offering guidance and support as they navigated the treacherous waters of his subconscious.

Yet, despite the progress made in unravelling the intricate web of darkness that had taken root within him, Samuel remained an enigma, a puzzle with pieces that seemed to shift and morph with each passing moment. Dr Stirling knew that the journey to understanding Samuel's true nature would be a long and arduous one, fraught with peril and uncertainty.

But he was determined to see it through, for he knew that within the depths of Samuel's troubled mind lay the key to unlocking the mysteries of Ravenwood Manor and the malevolent forces that lurked within its walls. And so, with unwavering resolve, Dr Stirling pressed on, ready to confront whatever darkness awaited them in the shadows.

One evening, as Samuel sat in the dimly lit room with Dr Stirling, he felt a presence, a dark energy that seemed to seep from the very walls. A voice whispered in the recesses of his mind, urging him to resist the efforts to break his bonds.

But Samuel knew that he couldn't continue down this path of darkness. He had seen the visions of his future, and the prospect of becoming an evil ruler filled him with dread.

He had to find a way to break free from the grip of the grimoire and the darkness that threatened to consume him. As Samuel grappled with his inner turmoil, Lady Eleanor consulted Professor Edward Sinclair, the expert in the occult.

Together, they scoured the hidden chamber beneath Ravenwood Manor, searching for a solution to free Samuel from the dark forces that bound him.

The items brought by the professor were a collection of ancient texts and artifacts, each holding a mysterious significance that hinted at a bygone era when magic and mysticism held sway over the world.

Among the texts were weathered scrolls and crumbling manuscripts, their pages adorned with intricate symbols and cryptic incantations. These ancient tomes contained knowledge that had been passed down through generations, their secrets guarded by those who sought to harness the power of the arcane.

The artifacts, on the other hand, were tangible relics of a time long past, each one imbued with a sense of ancient wisdom and mystic energy. There were talismans crafted from rare metals and precious gemstones, their surfaces etched with symbols of protection and power.

Other artifacts included ancient runes carved into stone tablets, their origins lost to the mists of time. These inscriptions held the key to unlocking the secrets of the universe, their meanings veiled in layers of symbolism and metaphor.

Together, these texts and artifacts formed a treasure trove of arcane knowledge, a window into a world where magic and mysticism were more than mere legends. They represented a link to a forgotten past, a time when the boundaries between the mundane and the supernatural were blurred, and the forces of darkness and light waged an eternal struggle for dominance.

He explained to Lady Eleanor that the grimoire Samuel had found was a gateway to a realm of malevolence, and it would take a formidable counterforce to sever its influence.

In the dimly lit chamber, surrounded by centuries-old books and arcane symbols, Lady Eleanor and Professor Sinclair embarked on a perilous journey. They conducted rituals to invoke protective spirits and invoked incantations to weaken the dark force's hold on Samuel.

The rituals to invoke protective spirits were elaborate ceremonies conducted with meticulous attention to detail. They involved the lighting of sacred candles, the burning of fragrant herbs and incense, and the chanting of ancient prayers passed down through generations. The participants would form a circle, their hands joined in solemn unity as they called upon the spirits of light to shield Samuel from harm.

As the incantations were spoken, the air crackled with energy, and the very ground beneath their feet seemed to pulse with power. The words themselves were a potent blend of ancient languages and secret symbols, each syllable infused with the strength of centuries-old knowledge. They resonated through the chamber like a chorus of voices from beyond the veil, their purpose to weaken the dark force's hold on Samuel and free him from its malevolent grasp.

With each incantation uttered, the darkness that had clouded Samuel's mind began to recede, replaced by a glimmer of light that shone with renewed hope. The participants could feel the weight of the oppressive presence lifting, replaced by an aura of peace and tranquillity that permeated the room.

But even as they performed these rituals, they knew that the battle was far from over. The dark forces that sought to claim Samuel's soul were powerful and relentless, and they would stop at nothing to achieve their twisted goals. It would take more than mere words and gestures to defeat them—it would take courage, determination, and unwavering faith in the power of light to triumph over darkness. And so, with hearts fortified and spirits renewed, they pressed on, ready to face whatever challenges lay ahead in their quest to save Samuel from his fate.

As they delved deeper into their mystical efforts, they could feel the grimoire's power pushing back, resisting their attempts to break its grip. The very foundations of Ravenwood Manor seemed to shake, and the presence of malevolence intensified.

Despite their best efforts, Lady Eleanor and Professor Sinclair could not fully sever the dark force's hold on Samuel. It was as though the grimoire possessed a sentience of its own, fighting back with an unholy determination.

Samuel, aware of their efforts, felt a renewed sense of conflict within himself. He had glimpsed the darkness that awaited him in his visions, and he knew that he had to resist its pull. But the allure of power and the sense of invincibility it offered were hard to resist.

Dr Stirling continued her sessions with Samuel, trying to reach the core of his being. She knew that only by confronting the source of his inner darkness could they hope to save him. Samuel's mind became a battleground, with his true self fighting to break free from the force that threatened to consume him.

As twilight descended upon Ravenwood Manor, casting long shadows across the ancient halls, Samuel Carrington found himself ensconced in a particularly intense session with Dr Stirling. The air in the dimly lit chamber was heavy with anticipation, as if the very walls themselves were holding their breath in anticipation of what was to come.

Samuel sat opposite Dr Stirling, his hands clenched into tight fists as he struggled to contain the tempest of emotions raging within him.

His brow furrowed in concentration, his features twisted in a mask of anguish as he grappled with the demons that lurked in the darkest recesses of his mind.

As Dr Stirling probed deeper into Samuel's psyche, his questions seemed to strike a nerve, igniting a spark of primal energy that simmered beneath the surface. With each passing moment, the tension in the room grew palpable, a coiled spring of anticipation ready to be unleashed at any moment.

And then, it happened—a surge of power unlike anything Samuel had ever experienced before coursed through his veins, setting every nerve ablaze with raw energy. The room trembled and shook, as if the very foundations of Ravenwood Manor were being tested by some unseen force.

The walls seemed to close in on Samuel, their oppressive weight bearing down on him like a suffocating blanket of darkness. He felt as if he were being swallowed whole by the shadows, consumed by the overwhelming tide of his own inner turmoil.

In that moment of chaos, Samuel's control slipped, and his powers surged forth with uncontrollable force. Objects in the room trembled and quaked, their forms twisting and distorting in the maelstrom of energy that surrounded him.

Dr Stirling watched in awe as Samuel's inner turmoil manifested in the physical world, his eyes wide with a mixture of fear and fascination. He knew that they had crossed a threshold into uncharted territory, delving deeper into the mysteries of Samuel's psyche than ever before.

But even as the room trembled, and the walls seemed to close in around them, Dr Stirling remained steadfast, his determination unyielding in the face of the chaos unfolding before him. For he knew that only by confronting the darkness within could Samuel ever hope to find the light.

Dr Stirling, undeterred by the chaos around her, pressed on with her questions. "Samuel, you have to fight this darkness within you. You are not a vessel for malevolence; you are a child who deserves love and a future filled with light."

Samuel, his face contorted with pain and inner conflict, shouted in frustration. "You don't understand! The power...it's intoxicating. I can shape the world to my will. I can have everything I desire."

As he spoke, a mirror on the wall shattered, its shards scattering across the room. Dr Stirling knew that she had touched a nerve, and she pushed further.

"But at what cost, Samuel? Is the pursuit of power worth losing yourself, your humanity?"

Samuel's eyes filled with tears, and he collapsed to the floor, his body racked with sobs. The darkness within him seemed to waver, its grip weakening for a moment.

In the wake of the intense session with Dr Stirling, Samuel began to question his path. The vision of his future, once alluring, now haunted him like a spectre. He had glimpsed the devastation he could unleash upon the world, and the thought filled him with dread.

Lady Eleanor and Sir Robert continued to support Samuel, their love for him unwavering despite the darkness that had threatened to tear their family apart. Dr Stirling's sessions had opened a door to his conscience, and Samuel yearned to break free from the force's hold.

But the grimoire, the source of his power, would not relinquish its grasp so easily. It whispered in the depths of his mind, promising him untold glory and dominion over all. Samuel knew that he had to find a way to destroy the cursed book and sever the connection once and for all.

Lady Eleanor and Professor Sinclair redoubled their efforts to find a way to rid Samuel of the grimoire's influence. They consulted ancient texts and sought guidance from spiritual leaders from around the world.

As the evening sun dipped below the horizon, casting long shadows across the study of Ravenwood Manor, Samuel and his companions found themselves immersed in their research, delving deeper into the mysteries of the ancient grimoire that had plagued them for so long. The air was heavy with anticipation, the flickering candlelight casting an ethereal glow over the centuries-old texts that lay scattered across the table.

With each turn of the page, they unearthed secrets, long forgotten, ancient incantations whispered by generations past in hushed tones. The words danced before their eyes, weaving a tapestry of mysticism and magic that held the key to their salvation.

And then, amidst the dusty tomes and weathered scrolls, they stumbled upon it—a centuries-old incantation, its words etched into the pages of an ancient manuscript with painstaking precision. As they read the words aloud, the air seemed to crackle with energy, the very fabric of reality bending to their will.

The incantation spoke of a power beyond comprehension, a force so ancient and so potent that it had the ability to bind even the darkest of entities. With each syllable uttered, they could feel the weight of centuries-old magic coursing through their veins, filling them with a sense of purpose and determination.

But it was not just the words themselves that held power—it was the intention behind them, the collective will of those who sought to banish the darkness that threatened to consume them. For in that moment, they were not just reciting a ritual—they were tapping into a force greater than themselves, drawing upon the very essence of the universe to achieve their goal.

And as the final words of the incantation echoed through the study, a sense of calm washed over them, a feeling of peace and tranquillity that had eluded them for so long. For they knew that they had finally found the key to containing the grimoire's force, to banishing the darkness that had plagued them for so long and restoring balance to the world once more.

As the incantation reached its crescendo, the grimoire's power waned, and its influence on Samuel began to weaken. He felt a surge of agony as the darkness within him fought against the binding spell.

In that moment of excruciating pain, Samuel saw the true extent of the grimoire's malevolence. It had promised him power and dominion, but it had stripped him of his humanity, turning him into a vessel of darkness. The visions of his future as a tyrant no longer held any allure.

With a final burst of energy, the incantation took hold, and the grimoire's force was sealed within a sacred artifact, a pendant of obsidian and silver. The room fell silent, and Samuel collapsed to the floor, free from the darkness that had gripped him for so long.

But the battle was far from over. The pendant containing the force had to be safeguarded, lest it fall into the wrong hands. Samuel, with his newfound clarity, knew that he had to take on the responsibility of protecting it. The Carrington family had faced the darkness within, and they were now united in their determination to ensure that it never returned to Ravenwood Manor.

UNVEILING THE TRUTH

The hidden chamber beneath Ravenwood Manor had become a sanctuary of sorts, a place where the forces of light and darkness had clashed in a battle for the soul of Samuel Carrington.

Now, with the force sealed within the obsidian and silver pendant, the chamber held a profound sense of stillness. Samuel, Lady Eleanor, Sir Robert, and Professor Edward Sinclair stood in the dimly lit chamber, the pendant containing the darkness resting on a pedestal at its centre. The air was heavy with the weight of the recent confrontation.

"I can't thank you all enough for what you've done," Samuel said, his voice filled with gratitude. "I was lost in the darkness, and you saved me."

Lady Eleanor embraced Samuel, tears of relief in her eyes.

"You are our son, Samuel, and we would do anything to protect you." Professor Sinclair, his gaze fixed on the pendant, spoke with a sense of solemnity. "The battle may be won, but the war is not over. We must ensure that the darkness sealed within this pendant never returns to threaten the world."

In the weeks that followed, Samuel took on the responsibility of safeguarding the pendant. He wore it around his neck at all times, a constant reminder of the darkness he had faced and the need to remain vigilant.

The Carrington family decided to keep the pendant within the hidden chamber, secured behind layers of protective spells and wards.

Professor Sinclair, with his expertise in the occult, oversaw the defences, ensuring that the evil force would remain contained.

Life at Ravenwood Manor began to return to a semblance of normalcy. Samuel resumed his studies, though now with a renewed sense of purpose. He had glimpsed the depths of his own darkness and was determined to use his powers for good.

But the darkness was not so easily vanquished. It whispered to Samuel in moments of solitude, tempting him with promises of power and dominion. He knew that he had to remain strong, for the force within the pendant was a constant reminder of the price of his choices.

One evening, as Samuel sat alone in his room, he felt a peculiar sensation, a tingling in the pendant that hung around his neck. He gazed at it with a sense of foreboding, and a voice echoed in the depths of his mind.

"Release me, Samuel," the voice hissed, its tone dripping with malice. "You cannot contain my power forever. Embrace the darkness, and you will know true power beyond your wildest dreams."

Samuel clutched the pendant, his knuckles white with determination.

"I will never let you be free," he replied, his voice firm. "I've seen the destruction you can cause, and I won't allow it to happen again."

The voice within the pendant grew furious, its whispers growing louder and more insistent. But Samuel remained resolute, his willpower unwavering.

As the days turned into weeks, Samuel's internal struggle with the darkness within the pendant continued. It seemed to intensify whenever he used his powers, a constant reminder of the force that lurked within.

One evening, as he practiced a spell under Professor Sinclair's guidance, the pendant grew warm against his chest. The professor noticed Samuel's discomfort and inquired about it.

"It's the pendant," Samuel explained, his brow furrowed. "It's reacting to my use of magic."

Professor Sinclair examined the pendant closely.

"It's as though the darkness within it is trying to break free. We must be cautious, Samuel. The containment spell is strong, but the force is relentless."

Samuel nodded, his eyes fixed on the pendant. He knew that the battle was far from over, and he had to remain vigilant to ensure that the darkness remained sealed.

As Samuel grappled with the presence of the pendant, Lady Eleanor and Sir Robert decided to seek guidance from a group of experts in the occult. They reached out to an ancient order of guardians who had dedicated their lives to containing dark forces and protecting the world from dark magic.

The guardians, led by a wise and enigmatic figure known as Master Elric, arrived at Ravenwood Manor. They examined the pendant with a sense of reverence recognising the force that lay within.

"Your family has faced a great challenge," Master Elric spoke with a voice that carried the weight of centuries. "The darkness within this pendant is a formidable adversary, but it can be controlled with the right measures."

Under Master Elric's guidance, the guardians performed a series of rituals to strengthen the containment spell on the pendant. They infused it with protective enchantments and wards that would make it nearly impervious to the force's attempts to break free.

With the pendant now fortified by the guardians' spells, Samuel felt a renewed sense of security. The force within it seemed to simmer beneath the surface, its attempts to break free growing less frequent.

Life at Ravenwood Manor returned to a semblance of normalcy once more. Samuel continued his studies and honed his magical abilities under the watchful eye of Professor Sinclair.

The Carrington family remained vigilant, knowing that the darkness could not be underestimated. But as the days turned into months, a sense of unease still lingered. Lady Eleanor couldn't shake the feeling that the darkness within the pendant was merely biding its time, waiting for an opportunity to strike back. She confided in Samuel one evening, her concern evident in her eyes.

"Samuel, we must remain vigilant," she cautioned. "The darkness within that pendant is relentless. We cannot afford to let our guard down."

Samuel nodded in agreement. He knew that the battle was far from over, and the force would always be a threat. The Carrington family had to remain united in their determination to keep the darkness at bay.

One evening, as a thick fog descended upon Ravenwood Manor, a knock sounded at the grand front door. The Carrington's exchanged puzzled glances, as they weren't expecting any visitors. Samuel went to answer the door, his senses on high alert.

As he swung the door open, a figure cloaked in shadow stood on the threshold. The stranger's face was hidden beneath the hood of their dark cloak, and their presence seemed to exude an aura of mystery.

"Who are you?" Samuel asked, his voice tinged with caution.

The stranger spoke with a voice that seemed to echo from the depths of time. "I am a seeker of knowledge, and I have come seeking answers."

Samuel, intrigued by the enigmatic visitor, invited them inside. The Carrington family gathered in the drawing room, where the stranger explained their purpose.

"I have heard of the pendant that contains a dark force," the stranger began. "I believe it holds a key to a greater mystery, one that could have far-reaching consequences."

The mysterious visitor, whose name was revealed to be Seraphina, had a knowledge of ancient lore and forbidden magic that surpassed even Professor Sinclair's expertise. She explained that the force within the pendant was not a singular entity but a fragment of a much greater darkness, a darkness that had existed for centuries.

"Long ago," Seraphina recounted, "there was a powerful sorcerer who sought to conquer the world with dark magic. His ambitions knew no bounds, and he cast a forbidden spell that shattered his own soul into fragments, each containing a portion of his malevolence."

Samuel listened in astonishment, realising that the darkness he had faced was not a random force but a part of a sorcerer's fractured soul.

Seraphina continued, "The pendant you possess contains one such fragment. But there are others scattered across the world, hidden in places of great significance. If these fragments were ever to be reunited, the sorcerer's malevolence would be unleashed upon the world, and chaos would reign."

The Carrington's, now aware of the true nature of the darkness they had faced, understood the gravity of the situation. They knew that they had to embark on a perilous quest to find and secure the remaining fragments of the sorcerer's soul before it could be reassembled.

The battle against darkness had taken a new and dangerous turn, and the fate of Ravenwood Manor and the world itself hung in the balance. The Carrington family, along with Seraphina, were now bound by a destiny that would lead them on a journey into the heart of darkness to prevent its resurgence.

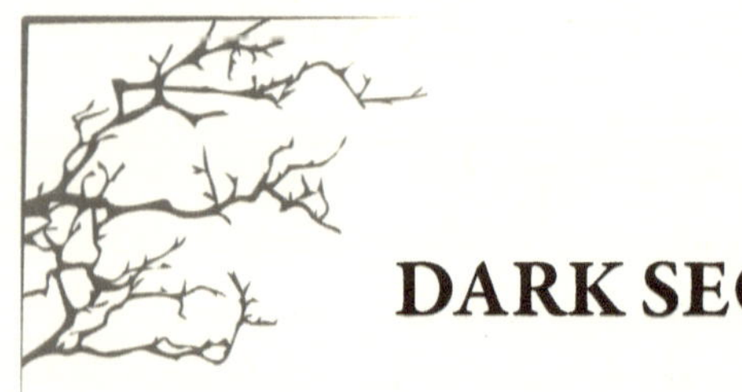

DARK SECRETS

As the Carrington family and Seraphina contemplated the magnitude of their new quest, they knew that finding and securing the remaining fragments of the sorcerer's soul would be a perilous journey. Each fragment was a source of great power, and in the wrong hands, they could unleash untold devastation upon the world.

Seraphina, with her extensive knowledge of ancient lore and forbidden magic, revealed that the fragments were bound to objects of significance, relics from the sorcerer's past. These objects had been scattered across the world, hidden away in places of historical and mystical importance.

Their first task was to uncover the locations of these objects. Samuel, Lady Eleanor, Sir Robert, and Professor Sinclair gathered in the library of Ravenwood Manor, poring over ancient texts and scrolls that held clues to the fragments' whereabouts.

"We must tread carefully," Seraphina warned. "The darkness will seek to thwart our efforts at every turn."

Samuel nodded, his determination unwavering. The fate of the world depended on their success. Their research led them to believe that the first fragment could be hidden within an ancient relic known as the "Chalice
of Shadows." Legend had it that the chalice had been used by the sorcerer in his darkest rituals, imbuing it with a portion of his malevolence.

The chalice was said to be hidden in the depths of the Blackwood Forest, a place shrouded in mystery and danger. Samuel, Lady Eleanor,

Sir Robert, Professor Sinclair, and Seraphina set out on their quest, armed with knowledge and determination.

The journey through the dense, ancient forest was fraught with peril. Eerie whispers seemed to emanate from the shadows, and the trees themselves appeared to watch their every move. But the Carrington's and Seraphina pressed on, guided by the faint aura of malevolence that surrounded the chalice.

After days of searching, they stumbled upon a hidden glen bathed in an otherworldly glow. At its centre stood a stone pedestal upon which rested the Chalice of Shadows. Samuel reached out to grasp it, his hand trembling with anticipation.

As Samuel lifted the Chalice of Shadows from its pedestal, a surge of dark energy coursed through him. The darkness within the chalice seemed to awaken, its presence more tangible than ever.

Seraphina stepped forward; her eyes fixed on the chalice.

"We must be careful," she cautioned. "The fragment within this object holds a portion of the sorcerer's malevolence. It will seek to corrupt those who touch it."

Samuel nodded, his determination unwavering. He knew that the darkness was a formidable adversary, but they couldn't allow it to deter their quest.

With the Chalice of Shadows secured in a protective container, the group made their way back through the Blackwood Forest. The eerie whispers and watchful trees seemed to recede, as though acknowledging their triumph.

Upon returning to Ravenwood Manor, they placed the Chalice of Shadows within the hidden chamber, alongside the pendant containing the first fragment. Two pieces of the sorcerer's soul had been secured, but the quest was far from over.

Their next lead pointed to an ancient amulet known as the "Eye of Oblivion," rumoured to be hidden in the labyrinthine catacombs beneath the city of Prague. The amulet was said to have been used by the sorcerer to manipulate time and perception.

The Carrington family, along with Seraphina, embarked on a journey to the historic city of Prague. The catacombs were a labyrinth of dark tunnels and chambers, filled with centuries old secrets and the restless spirits of the past.

As they descended into the depths of the catacombs, the air grew cold and oppressive. Strange symbols adorned the walls, and faint whispers echoed through the passages. The Eye of Oblivion was rumoured to be hidden deep within the catacombs, guarded by traps and ancient curses.

They had to rely on their wits and Seraphina's knowledge of arcane symbols to navigate the treacherous maze. The force within the amulet seemed to grow stronger the closer they came to their goal, its presence a constant reminder of the danger they faced.

After hours of navigating the twisting catacombs, the group finally reached a chamber that held the elusive "Eye of Oblivion." It rested on a stone pedestal at the centre of the room, bathed in an eerie, otherworldly light.

As the group stood before the pedestal, their eyes fixed on the elusive "Eye of Oblivion," a tense silence hung in the air, broken only by the soft whisper of their breath echoing off the ancient stone walls. Each member of the party felt the weight of the moment pressing down upon them, the gravity of their mission looming large in their minds.

Samuel, his gaze steady and unwavering, approached the amulet with caution, his senses alert to the dark energy that pulsed within it. He could feel the power emanating from the artifact, a palpable force that seemed to reach out to him with malevolent intent. Yet, despite the overwhelming sense of foreboding that washed over him, he knew that he had no choice but to press on.

As his hand hovered over the amulet, a surge of dark energy coursed through Samuel's veins, sending shivers down his spine.

Visions of twisted time and distorted reality flashed before his eyes, threatening to engulf him in a maelstrom of chaos. But he gritted his teeth and fought to maintain his grip on reality, refusing to succumb to the madness that threatened to consume him.

Meanwhile, Seraphina, her eyes blazing with determination, began to chant an incantation, her voice rising in a melodic cadence that filled the chamber with a sense of power and purpose.

"By the ancient powers that bind, I call upon the spirits of light to shine.

Let darkness yield and light prevail, As we break the chains of this dark veil.

From shadows deep and depths untold, I summon strength, both brave and bold.

With every word and every breath, We banish darkness, conquer death.

Let the forces of evil fade away, As we stand firm and do not sway.

With magic old and wisdom true, We free the captive, break the rue."

The ancient words echoed off the stone walls, weaving a tapestry of magic that sought to weaken the amulet's defences and break its hold over the group.

As her incantation reached its crescendo, the chamber seemed to tremble, the very air crackling with arcane energy. Ancient curses were lifted, and the force that had held the Eye of Oblivion in its thrall began to wane, its grip loosening with each passing moment.

With a final, resolute effort, Samuel reached out and secured the amulet, his hand closing around it with a sense of grim determination. Its energy had been subdued, its power contained once more within the confines of the artifact. And as the group made their way back through the twisting catacombs, their triumph was a testament to their unwavering resolve in the face of darkness.

Upon returning to Ravenwood Manor, the Eye of Oblivion was placed within the hidden chamber, alongside the Chalice of Shadows and the pendant. Three fragments of the sorcerer's soul had been secured, but the quest was far from over.

Their next lead pointed to an artifact known as the "Mirror of Desolation," said to be hidden deep within the ruins of an ancient temple in the jungles of South America. The mirror was rumoured to have the power to manipulate perception and sow discord among those who gazed into it.

The Carrington family, along with Seraphina and a local guide, embarked on a journey to the distant jungles, where they would face not only the perils of the wilderness but also the force that guarded the mirror.

As they ventured deeper into the jungle, the air grew thick with humidity, and the sounds of wildlife surrounded them.

The ruins of the ancient temple were hidden among the dense foliage, a testament to a civilisation long gone. But the mirror's power, they knew, was a force to be reckoned with, and they had to tread carefully as they approached their next destination.

The Carrington family, Seraphina and the guide ventured deeper into the dense jungles of South America, guided by ancient maps and lore that pointed the way to the ruins of the temple rumoured to house the "Mirror of Desolation." The lush foliage and exotic wildlife seemed to conceal the secrets of the past.

As they reached the heart of the jungle, they found themselves standing before the overgrown remains of the ancient temple. The stone structure was adorned with intricate carvings that told the story of a forgotten civilisation.

The mirror was said to be hidden within the temple's inner sanctum, a place shrouded in mystery and guarded by the force that resided within the artifact. The group entered the temple cautiously, torchlight flickering as they descended deeper into its depths.

As they reached the inner sanctum, a chilling presence filled the air. The room was adorned with ornate symbols and ancient relics, but at its centre stood the "Mirror of Desolation," a tall, obsidian-framed looking glass.

The mirror seemed to radiate an unsettling energy, and the Carrington's felt the weight of the force that resided within it. Samuel approached the mirror cautiously, his reflection distorted as he gazed into its depths.

The force, aware of their presence, lashed out with a surge of dark energy. The room trembled as the mirror's power sought to manipulate their perceptions and sow discord among them.

Seraphina, her voice unwavering, began to chant an incantation to weaken the mirror's defences. She called upon protective spirits and ancient guardians to aid them in their quest.

"By the spirits of old and guardians untold, I call upon thee, protectors bold.

From realms beyond and worlds unseen, Come forth now, to intervene.

With steadfast hearts and unwavering might, We banish darkness, restore the light.

Let ancient forces rise and stand, To aid us in our noble command.

Mirror of darkness, be bound and contained, By the powers of light, thy influence restrained.

We stand united, resolute and true, To overcome the darkness that once grew.

With each word spoken, with each verse sung, We weaken thy hold, till thy power is undone.

Protective spirits, guardians divine, Join us now, in this noble design.

For we are warriors of light, champions of the day, And in our hands, darkness shall not hold sway.

With courage and conviction, we shall prevail, And banish the shadows with our incantation's tale."

The force fought back with a relentless determination, but the group's resolve remained unshaken. They had faced darkness before and emerged victorious.

Samuel, with newfound clarity, reached out to grasp the mirror. Its dark energy waned, and the room fell silent once more.

With the "Mirror of Desolation" secured, the group made their way back through the jungle, their triumph a testament to their determination. The force within the mirror had been subdued, but they knew that their quest was far from over.

Upon returning to Ravenwood Manor, they placed the mirror within the hidden chamber, alongside the other fragments of the sorcerer's soul. Four pieces had been secured, but they still had a long journey ahead.

Seraphina revealed that their next lead pointed to an ancient scroll known as the "Scroll of Shadows," hidden within the archives of a secluded monastery in the Himalayas. The scroll was said to contain forbidden knowledge and incantations of great power.

The Carrington family, along with Seraphina, prepared for their next expedition to the distant mountains, where they would face not only the physical challenges of the Himalayas but also the force that guarded the scroll.

As they embarked on their journey, the knowledge that they were one step closer to preventing the resurgence of the sorcerer's soul fuelled their determination. They would confront the darkness, uncover its secrets, and safeguard the world from its devastating power.

THE MALEVOLENT POWER

The Carrington family and Seraphina embarked on a perilous journey to the distant Himalayan mountains, where they sought the elusive "Scroll of Shadows." The ancient scroll was rumoured to contain forbidden knowledge and incantations of great power, making it a coveted artifact for those who sought to wield darkness.

The journey through the rugged terrain of the Himalayas was treacherous, as they navigated steep cliffs, unpredictable weather, and the thinning air of high altitudes. The majestic snow-capped peaks loomed in the distance, their beauty contrasting with the danger that lay ahead.

As they trekked deeper into the mountains, the group couldn't help but feel the force that resided within the scroll drawing closer, its presence growing stronger with each step. The darkness would not relinquish its hold on the artifact without a fight.

After days of challenging travel, the Carrington's and Seraphina reached the secluded monastery nestled within the Himalayan peaks. The ancient structure stood as a testament to centuries of devotion and seclusion.

The monastery's archives were rumoured to house the "Scroll of Shadows," safeguarded by generations of monks who understood the dangers of the dark knowledge contained within.

The group was welcomed by the monastery's abbot, a wise and serene figure named Brother Tenzin. "We seek the 'Scroll of Shadows,'" Samuel explained to Brother Tenzin, his tone respectful.

"We are aware of its power and the responsibility it carries." Brother Tenzin nodded; his eyes filled with understanding. He led them to the monastery's archives, a chamber filled with countless scrolls and tomes, each holding a piece of ancient wisdom.

As they searched through the archives, the force within the monastery seemed to awaken. Shadows danced along the walls, and an eerie chill filled the air.

"We are not alone," Seraphina whispered, her senses attuned to the presence of darkness.

Suddenly, the shadows coalesced into a sinister form, taking on a spectral shape that seemed both ethereal and creepy. The entity, driven by the darkness that permeated the scrolls, attacked with a relentless fury.

The Carrington family and Seraphina stood their ground, invoking protective spells and ancient incantations to ward off the entity. They all read from an ancient scroll:

"By the light of the moon and the strength of the sun, We call upon forces, our battles to be won.

With hearts united and spirits pure, We banish darkness, forevermore.

Ancient guardians, spirits of the land, Stand with us now, lend us your hand.

With shields of light and swords of truth, Protect us from the shadows, from the dark's cruel ruse.

Let our words be as a barrier, firm and strong, Against the evils that seek to do us wrong.

By the power of the ancients, by the strength of our will, We repel the darkness, our resolve unyielding still.

With each invocation, with each sacred verse, We strengthen our defences, for better or for worse.

No harm shall befall us, no fear shall hold sway, For we are protected, now and every day."

The battle between light and darkness raged within the archives of the monastery.

The struggle against the entity continued, each member of the group channelling their magic and resolve to protect the sacred knowledge contained within the archives.

As the battle reached its climax, Samuel, with determination in his eyes, made a crucial discovery. He spotted a scroll adorned with dark symbols and intricate incantations, unmistakably the "Scroll of Shadows." It lay protected beneath layers of ancient warding spells.

With the entity momentarily subdued, Samuel reached out and carefully retrieved the scroll. Its dark energy pulsed within his grasp, but he knew that they had to secure it to prevent its power from falling into the wrong hands.

Seraphina, her incantations reaching a crescendo, cast a binding spell on the entity, trapping it within a protective barrier. The entity let out a furious howl, its spectral form writhing in frustration.

With the "Scroll of Shadows" in their possession, the group made a hasty retreat from the archives of the monastery. The entity, imprisoned within the protective barrier, lashed out with one final, desperate attempt to escape.

The monastery's abbot, Brother Tenzin, stood at the entrance, his gaze filled with a mixture of gratitude and sorrow.

"May you safeguard the scroll's power," he said in a solemn tone. "But be wary of the darkness it contains."

The group descended from the mountains, their journey back to Ravenwood Manor filled with a sense of urgency. The force within the "Scroll of Shadows" would not rest, and they knew that the darkness would seek to reclaim its lost power.

Upon returning to Ravenwood Manor, the "Scroll of Shadows" was placed within the hidden chamber, alongside the other fragments of the sorcerer's soul. Five pieces had been secured, but the quest was far from over.

Seraphina began to decipher the ancient incantations and forbidden knowledge contained within the scroll. She uncovered dark secrets and powerful spells that had been hidden away for centuries.

"The sorcerer's ambitions were boundless," Seraphina explained to the Carrington's. "He sought to wield dark magic to reshape the world according to his desires. The scroll contains the means to manipulate reality and control the minds of others."

The Carrington's understood the gravity of their mission. The sorcerer's soul had been shattered, but his malevolence remained a potent threat. They had to remain vigilant and continue their quest to safeguard the fragments of darkness before they could be reunited and unleash untold chaos upon the world.

UNLEASHING THE DARKNESS

With the "Scroll of Shadows" secured within the hidden chamber at Ravenwood Manor, the Carrington family and Seraphina delved deeper into their quest to locate the remaining fragments of the sorcerer's soul.

Their next lead pointed to an ancient talisman known as the "Talisman of Torment." It was said to be hidden within the catacombs beneath the city of Venice, Italy. The talisman had the power to inflict torment and suffering upon its victims, making it a formidable weapon in the wrong hands.

The group embarked on a journey to the historic city of Venice, where they knew that the catacombs held secrets and dangers of their own. As they navigated the winding canals and labyrinthine streets of the city, the weight of history and mystery surrounded them.

In the archives of an ancient Venetian library, they uncovered a manuscript that detailed the location of the talisman within the catacombs. The document spoke of a hidden passage that led to the depths of the underground labyrinth; a passage known only to a select few.

Armed with the knowledge of the hidden passage, the Carrington's and Seraphina descended into the labyrinthine catacombs beneath Venice. The air grew damp and suffused with the scent of old stone and secrets long buried.

Their path took them through narrow tunnels and chambers adorned with ancient symbols and cryptic inscriptions. The catacombs were a maze of darkness, where echoes of the past seemed to linger, and shadows danced along the walls.

As they ventured deeper into the underground maze, the force that guarded the "Talisman of Torment" grew stronger. Whispers of despair and torment filled the air, a chilling reminder of the talisman's power.

The group reached a chamber deep within the catacombs, where a pedestal stood at its centre. Upon the pedestal rested the "Talisman of Torment," a dark and foreboding artifact adorned with twisted symbols.

As Samuel reached out to secure the talisman, the force within it awakened with a vengeance. The chamber shook, and the shadows seemed to coalesce into a grotesque form.

The guardian of the talisman, a spectral entity fuelled by torment and suffering, materialised before them. It unleashed waves of anguish and despair, attempting to weaken their resolve.

Seraphina, her voice filled with determination, began to chant an incantation to ward off the guardian. She called upon protective spirits and ancient wards to shield the group from the torment that assailed them.

"By spirits ancient, protectors bold, I call upon thee, now unfold.

With shields of light and wards of might, Guard us now, through darkest night.

Let ancient guardians rise and stand, To shield us from the torments planned.

By the power of the old and wise, Protect us now, from demise.

Ward off the darkness, banish the fear, Let no harm come near, let us be clear.

With every word, with every plea, Shield us now, so mote it be.

By spirits of light and guardians true, Protect us now, till the danger is through.

With hearts united, we stand tall, Warded by magic, we shall not fall."

The battle with the guardian raged on, as the group channelled their magic and determination to withstand its onslaught. The guardian, driven by the power of the talisman, lashed out with illusions of suffering and despair.

Samuel, with the talisman in his grasp, struggled to maintain his focus. The torment inflicted upon him by the guardian's illusions threatened to overwhelm him.

But the Carrington's and Seraphina stood together, their bond of family and their shared mission giving them the strength to resist. They knew that the talisman's power had to be contained to prevent it from falling into the wrong hands.

With a final, resolute effort, Samuel secured the "Talisman of Torment," its energy waning as the guardian's spectral form dissipated into nothingness.

As they made their way back through the catacombs, the group carried the "Talisman of Torment" with them, knowing that its power was both a weapon and a burden.

Upon returning to Ravenwood Manor, they placed the talisman within the hidden chamber, alongside the other fragments of the sorcerer's soul. Six pieces had been secured, but their quest was far from over.

Seraphina continued to decipher the dark knowledge contained within the "Scroll of Shadows" and the talisman. The sorcerer's legacy was a tapestry of darkness and forbidden magic, and they were determined to unravel its secrets.

The group understood that the sorcerer's ambitions had known no bounds, and the fragments of his soul were a testament to his malevolence. They had to remain vigilant and continue their quest to safeguard the fragments before they could be reunited and unleash untold chaos upon the world.

Their next lead pointed to an ancient talisman known as the "Talisman of Torment." It was said to be hidden within the catacombs beneath the city of Venice, Italy. The talisman had the power to inflict torment and suffering upon its victims, making it a formidable weapon in the wrong hands.

The group embarked on a journey to the historic city of Venice, where they knew that the catacombs held secrets and dangers of their own. As they navigated the winding canals and labyrinthine streets of the city, the weight of history and mystery surrounded them.

In the archives of an ancient Venetian library, they uncovered a manuscript that detailed the location of the talisman within the catacombs. The document spoke of a hidden passage that led to the depths of the underground labyrinth, a passage known only to a select few.

"In the shadows of Venetian lore, beneath the city's ancient streets, lies a labyrinth of passages and chambers, a realm forgotten by time itself. It is here, amidst the winding tunnels and hidden alcoves, that the talisman of light resides, a beacon of hope in the face of darkness.

To find it, seek ye the hidden passage, concealed from prying eyes by the veils of secrecy. It is a path known only to those who dare to tread where others fear to go—a journey fraught with peril, yet filled with the promise of salvation.

Descend into the depths of the underground labyrinth, guided by the flickering light of your courage and the whispers of ancient spirits. Navigate the twisting corridors and treacherous traps, for only those with the strength of will and the purity of heart shall succeed in their quest.

And when at last you stand before the talisman, let not fear nor doubt cloud your resolve. For with each step taken and each challenge overcome, you draw closer to unlocking the power that lies dormant within.

Go forth, brave souls, and may the light of the talisman guide you on your journey, illuminating the path to victory over the forces of darkness that seek to consume us all."

As they made their way back through the catacombs, the group carried the "Talisman of Torment" with them, knowing that its power was both a weapon and a burden. The force within the talisman had been subdued, but they understood the weight of the darkness it represented.

FAMILY IN PERIL

In the dimly lit study of Ravenwood Manor, the Carrington family gathered around a large, ornate table. The room was adorned with ancient tapestries and shelves filled with books on magic, history, and the occult. Seraphina stood at the head of the table, her eyes filled with both concern and determination.

"Each fragment we secure brings us closer to preventing the sorcerer's soul from reuniting," Seraphina began, her voice carrying the weight of their mission. "But we must remain vigilant. The darkness seeks to reclaim its power."

Samuel, Lady Eleanor, Sir Robert, and Professor Sinclair nodded in agreement. They knew that their quest was far from over, and the evil that lurked within the fragments of the sorcerer's soul would stop at nothing to thwart their efforts.

"Our next lead points to an ancient artifact known as the 'Shroud of Shadows,'" Seraphina continued. "It is said to be hidden within the catacombs beneath the city of Paris, France. The shroud has the power to cloak its wearer in darkness, rendering them invisible to both the eye and magical detection."

With their sights set on Paris, the Carrington family and Seraphina made preparations for their journey. The City of Lights was known for its history, culture, and enchanting charm, but beneath its bustling streets lay secrets and mysteries of a different kind.

As they arrived in Paris, the group marvelled at the iconic landmarks that adorned the city—the Eiffel Tower, the Louvre, and the Notre-Dame Cathedral. Yet, they knew that their true destination lay beneath the cobblestone streets.

The catacombs of Paris were a labyrinth of tunnels and chambers that held the remains of countless souls. It was within this subterranean realm that they believed the "Shroud of Shadows" was hidden.

The Carrington's and Seraphina ventured into the catacombs beneath Paris, their footsteps echoing through the dimly lit tunnels. Skulls and bones were stacked along the walls, a macabre reminder of the catacombs' grim purpose.

Their search led them deeper into the labyrinthine passages, where the air grew thick with the weight of the past. Strange symbols and markings adorned the walls, hinting at the catacombs' hidden history.

As they navigated the maze-like catacombs, they couldn't shake the feeling of being watched. Shadows flickered at the edges of their vision, and eerie whispers filled the air. The force that guarded the "Shroud of Shadows" was ever-present, its presence growing stronger with each step.

In a chamber deep within the catacombs, the Carrington's and Seraphina came upon a stone pedestal. Upon the pedestal lay the "Shroud of Shadows," a dark and ethereal garment that seemed to defy the laws of reality.

Samuel approached the shroud cautiously, fully aware of the force that resided within it. As he reached out to secure the artifact, the chamber trembled, and the shadows coalesced into a formidable guardian.

The guardian of the shroud, a spectral entity cloaked in darkness, materialised before them. It possessed the power of invisibility and sought to use it against its intruders.

Seraphina, her voice unwavering, began to chant an incantation to ward off the guardian. She called upon ancient protective spells and invoked the power of light to pierce the darkness that surrounded them.

"By ancient spells and protective wards, I call upon thee, defenders of the light.

With voices raised and hearts ablaze, We banish darkness from our sight.

Let the power of light pierce the veil, And scatter shadows with its radiant might.

From realms beyond and worlds unseen, We call forth the dawn to end the night.

Protective spirits, guardians divine, Stand with us now, your strength entwined.

With every word, with every breath, We cast aside the darkness, conquer death.

Let no fear nor doubt hold sway, For we are warriors of the light, come what may.

With courage in our hearts and light as our guide, We ward off darkness, let it be denied.

By the power of ancient spells and the light's pure flame, We ward off the guardian, we stake our claim.

With voices raised and spirits strong, We banish darkness, forever long."

The battle with the guardian raged on, as the group channelled their magic and determination to withstand its onslaught. The guardian, empowered by the "Shroud of Shadows," attempted to cloak itself in darkness and strike from the shadows.

Samuel, with the shroud in his grasp, struggled to maintain his focus. The guardian's invisibility made it a formidable adversary, and their battle became a test of skill and will.

But the Carrington's and Seraphina stood together, their resolve unshaken. They knew that the shroud's power had to be contained to prevent it from being used for purposes. With a final, resolute effort, Samuel secured the "Shroud of Shadows," its evil energy waning as the guardian's spectral form dissipated into nothingness.

With the "Shroud of Shadows" in their possession, the group made their way back through the catacombs, their triumph tinged with a sense of unease. The evil within the shroud had been subdued, but they understood the potential for its power to wreak havoc.

As they ascended from the depths of the catacombs and returned to the streets of Paris, they couldn't shake the feeling that they were being watched. The sorcerer's presence seemed to linger, its influence casting a shadow over their every move. They knew that their mission was far from over, and the darkness would continue to seek retribution.

Upon returning to Ravenwood Manor, they placed the "Shroud of Shadows" within the hidden chamber, alongside the other fragments of the sorcerer's soul. Seven pieces had been secured, but the sorcerer's legacy remained a potent threat.

Seraphina continued to decipher the dark incantations and forbidden knowledge contained within the shroud. It held secrets of invisibility and deception, powers that could be harnessed for both good and evil.

As Seraphina delved deeper into the shroud's secrets, she uncovered a sinister revelation. The sorcerer's intentions had gone beyond the mere accumulation of power. He had sought to manipulate reality itself, to bend it to his will and reshape the world according to his desires.

"His ambitions knew no bounds," Seraphina explained to the Carrington's. "The 'Shroud of Shadows' holds the power to alter perception and reality. With it, one could become invisible to the world, slipping through the cracks of existence."

The group understood the gravity of their mission. The fragments of the sorcerer's soul were not just sources of power; they were keys to unlocking the darkest of magic. The sorcerer's legacy was a tapestry of darkness and forbidden spells that could bring untold chaos to the world if left unchecked.

As the Carrington family and Seraphina pondered their next move, a chilling message arrived in the form of an ancient scroll. It bore a warning written in cryptic runes, a message from an unknown source.

"The darkness stirs," Seraphina translated the message. "It seeks to reunite, to reclaim its full power. You must hasten your quest, for the sorcerer's influence grows stronger."

The warning filled the room with an ominous air. The group knew that they were in a race against time, and the force they faced was cunning and relentless. With renewed determination, they set their sights on their next lead—a legendary amulet known as the "Amulet of Desolation."

It was said to be hidden within the treacherous depths of the Amazon rainforest, where dangers both natural and supernatural awaited.

The Carrington family and Seraphina knew that their journey into the heart of the jungle would test their limits and pit them against the sorcerer's influence once more. As they prepared to leave Ravenwood Manor, the weight of their mission hung heavily in the air.

The sorcerer's legacy was a shadow that loomed over them, but they would not falter. They were determined to safeguard the fragments of darkness and protect the world from the chaos that threatened to engulf it.

The journey into the Amazon rainforest was an arduous and perilous one. The dense foliage, treacherous terrain, and sweltering heat tested the resolve of the Carrington family and Seraphina. They knew that the "Amulet of Desolation" was hidden deep within the heart of this untamed wilderness.

As they ventured further into the jungle, they encountered exotic wildlife, ancient ruins, and the whispers of indigenous tribes who spoke of the amulet's power. The Amazon rainforest was a realm where the line between reality and myth blurred, and the darkness they sought to contain seemed to intertwine with the very essence of the jungle.

Deep within the heart of the rainforest, the Carrington's and Seraphina reached a hidden temple shrouded in mystery. The temple was adorned with intricate carvings and adorned with symbols that hinted at the amulet's power.

At the temple's entrance, they faced guardians—ancient spirits bound to protect the "Amulet of Desolation." These spectral entities, once human, had been ensnared by the sorcerer's dark magic, their existence forever tied to the amulet's secrets.

A tense standoff ensued as the guardians confronted the intruders. Their ethereal forms exuded an aura of despair and desolation, a reflection of the amulet's power. The guardians would not relinquish their charge without a battle.

The battle with the guardians of the amulet was a clash of wills and magic. The spectral entities summoned illusions of desolation and sorrow, attempting to weaken the resolve of the intruders.

Samuel Carrington stood at the forefront of a gathering storm, his eyes blazing with determination as he prepared to secure the coveted "Amulet of Desolation." Beside him stood Lady Eleanor and Sir Robert, their faces etched with resolve as they summoned forth their inner strength to aid in their quest.

Professor Sinclair, the esteemed scholar and guardian of arcane knowledge, stood poised at the ready, his mind a repository of ancient spells and protective magic passed down through generations.

As Samuel reached out to grasp the amulet, a surge of dark energy coursed through him, threatening to overwhelm his senses. But he drew upon the protective magic he had learned from Seraphina, weaving a barrier of light around himself and his companions to shield them from harm. The air crackled with energy as their combined efforts created a shimmering aura of protection, warding off the malevolent forces that sought to thwart their advance.

Lady Eleanor and Sir Robert, their hearts filled with determination, stood by Samuel's side, their unwavering resolve bolstering his own. With each step forward, they drew upon their inner strength, channelling it into a formidable shield against the encroaching darkness. Together, they formed a united front against the looming threat, their collective will a beacon of hope in the face of adversity.

Meanwhile, Professor Sinclair delved into his extensive knowledge of ancient spells, his mind a wellspring of arcane wisdom passed down through generations of scholars and mystics. Drawing upon the teachings of ages past, he summoned forth the power of forgotten incantations and protective wards, weaving them into a tapestry of magic that enveloped the group in its protective embrace.

With each word spoken and each gesture made, the chamber thrummed with the energy of ancient magic, its echoes reverberating through the stone walls and into the very heart of the amulet itself. The air crackled with anticipation as Samuel and his companions pressed forward, their determination unwavering despite the odds stacked against them.

And as they stood on the precipice of victory, surrounded by the pulsing energy of their combined efforts, they knew that they were ready to face whatever challenges lay ahead. For in that moment, they were not just individuals, but a united force of light against the encroaching darkness, bound together by their shared purpose and unyielding resolve.

As the group made their way back through the Amazon rainforest, the force within the amulet seemed to seep into their very souls. The amulet was a repository of despair and desolation, and its influence weighed heavily on their minds.

In a climactic battle against the guardians of the amulet, Samuel Carrington and his companions employed a combination of strategic prowess, mystical knowledge, and unwavering determination to emerge victorious. As the guardians unleashed their formidable powers in a bid to protect the ancient artifact, the group faced a daunting challenge unlike any they had encountered before.

Lady Eleanor, drawing upon her innate strength and resilience, engaged the guardians head-on, her sword flashing in the dim light as she parried their blows with expert precision. With each swing of her blade, she struck fear into the hearts of their adversaries, her courage serving as a rallying cry for her companions.

Sir Robert, his muscles bulging with the effort of battle, stood firm at Lady Eleanor's side, his shield raised high to deflect the onslaught of attacks directed their way. With unwavering determination, he met the guardians blow for blow, his unwavering resolve bolstering the group's defences and inspiring hope in their hearts.

Meanwhile, Professor Sinclair, the scholarly guardian of ancient knowledge, called upon the arcane arts to aid in their struggle. With a wave of his hand and a murmured incantation, he unleashed a torrent of mystical energy upon the guardians, weaving spells of binding and containment to immobilise their adversaries and tip the scales in their favour.

As the battle raged on, Samuel Carrington, fueled by a fierce determination to claim the amulet, unleashed the full extent of his powers upon the guardians. Drawing upon the protective magic he had learned from Seraphina and channelling it into a devastating onslaught, he struck at the heart of their foes with a relentless fury that left them reeling.

With each passing moment, the guardians found themselves outmatched and outmanoeuvred by the combined might of Samuel and his companions. Their defences weakened, their resolve faltered, until at last, they were forced to concede defeat in the face of overwhelming odds.

And as the final blow fell, the guardians crumbled before the relentless onslaught of Samuel and his companions, their forms dissolving into wisps of smoke that vanished into the ether. With the guardians vanquished and the path to the amulet clear, Samuel and his companions stood victorious, their triumph a testament to their courage, determination, and unwavering resolve in the face of adversity.

Upon their return to Ravenwood Manor, they placed the "Amulet of Desolation" within the hidden chamber, alongside the other fragments of the sorcerer's soul. Eight pieces had been secured, but their quest was far from over. Seraphina continued to decipher the dark incantations and forbidden knowledge contained within the amulet. It held the power to invoke despair and desolation, to plunge the world into an unending abyss of sorrow.

The Carrington's and Seraphina knew that the sorcerer's influence was growing stronger with each fragment they secured. They had to remain vigilant and continue their quest to safeguard the fragments before they could be reunited and unleash untold chaos upon the world.

As they gathered around the hidden chamber, the weight of their mission hung heavily in the air. The sorcerer's legacy was a shadow that loomed over them, but they would not waver in their resolve. The fate of the world rested in their hands, and they were determined to protect it from the darkness that threatened to consume it.

The Carrington family and Seraphina knew that the sorcerer's influence was growing stronger with each fragment they secured. The fragments, each holding a piece of the sorcerer's dark soul, were like beacons calling out to the darkness.

As they delved deeper into the "Scroll of Shadows" and the artifacts they had collected, a realisation dawned upon them. The sorcerer's ultimate plan was not merely to reclaim his power; it was to merge the fragments and unleash a cataclysmic event that would plunge the world into eternal darkness.

"The convergence of these fragments will be the key," Seraphina explained solemnly. "When reunited, the sorcerer's soul will become whole once more, and his power will be beyond imagination."

Their quest now led them to the ancient city of Cairo, where they sought the "Crown of Eclipse," the final fragment of the sorcerer's soul. This dark artifact was rumoured to be hidden deep within the chambers of the Great Pyramid, where it had remained undisturbed for centuries.

As they ventured into the heart of the pyramid, the air grew heavy with the weight of history. Hieroglyphics adorned the walls, telling the story of the sorcerer's dark deeds and his quest for ultimate power.

In the heart of the pyramid, they reached a chamber bathed in an eerie, otherworldly glow. There, atop a pedestal, rested the "Crown of Eclipse," a sinister artifact that seemed to absorb the very light around it.

Samuel approached the "Crown of Eclipse" with caution, aware of the force it contained. As he reached out to secure the final fragment, the chamber trembled, and the shadows within the pyramid came to life.

The sorcerer's presence manifested in a spectral form, his eyes filled with malice and his voice dripping with venom. He then spoke of his grand plan to merge the fragments and plunge the world into eternal darkness, where he would reign as the ultimate sorcerer.

Seraphina, her voice filled with defiance, began to chant an incantation to weaken the sorcerer's spectral form. She called upon the ancient magic of Egypt, invoking the power of Ra and Osiris to thwart the sorcerer's resurgence.

"By the power of Ra, sun god of the ancient sands, I call upon thee to lend us thy guiding hands.

With rays of light and flames of divine might, We banish darkness, we banish night.

Osiris, lord of the underworld's domain, Hearken to our call, break the sorcerer's chain.

With sceptre raised and ankh in hand, We drive back darkness, we make our stand.

Ancient spirits, guardians of the Nile's flow, Stand with us now, let your power show.

With every word, with every plea, We weaken the sorcerer, set him free.

Let the light of Ra pierce the gloom, And dispel the shadows that seek to consume.

By the power of Egypt's ancient lore, We banish darkness, forevermore.

By the power of Ra and Osiris' grace, We cast out darkness from this sacred place.

With voices raised and spirits strong, We vanquish darkness, we right the wrong."

In the dimly lit chamber, Seraphina stood at the forefront of the group, her voice resolute as she chanted the ancient incantation. Her words carried the weight of centuries, resonating with the power of the gods themselves as she called upon the magic of Egypt to weaken the sorcerer's spectral form.

As she spoke, the air seemed to crackle with energy, and a faint golden glow surrounded her, illuminating the chamber with an ethereal light. The words of the incantation echoed off the stone walls, filling the room with a sense of ancient power and mysticism.

Behind Seraphina, Lady Eleanor and Sir Robert stood at the ready, their weapons drawn and their eyes fixed on the swirling darkness that enveloped the sorcerer. With each word of the incantation, they felt a surge of determination coursing through their veins, bolstering their resolve to defeat the malevolent entity once and for all.

Professor Sinclair, the scholarly guardian of arcane knowledge, watched intently as Seraphina channelled the magic of Egypt, his mind racing with the possibilities of what they could achieve. With each passing moment, he felt a sense of awe and reverence for the ancient rituals unfolding before him, knowing that they held the key to victory against their spectral foe.

As the incantation reached its crescendo, the chamber seemed to tremble with the power of the gods, and a brilliant flash of light erupted from Seraphina's outstretched hands. The sorcerer recoiled, his spectral form writhing in agony as the ancient magic washed over him, weakening his hold on the mortal realm.

But even as the sorcerer faltered, his dark power surged forth in a final, desperate attempt to break free from the bonds of the incantation. Shadows danced and twisted around him, threatening to overwhelm the group with their malevolent force.

Undeterred, Seraphina pressed on, her voice unwavering as she continued to chant the incantation with renewed determination. With each word spoken, the light grew brighter, pushing back the encroaching darkness and banishing the sorcerer's spectral form from their midst.

And as the last echoes of the incantation faded into the ether, the chamber fell silent once more, save for the steady breathing of the group as they stood victorious against the forces of darkness. With the sorcerer weakened and the ancient magic of Egypt on their side, they knew that they had taken a crucial step forward in their quest to save the world from impending doom.

Samuel, with the "Crown of Eclipse" in his grasp, felt the weight of the sorcerer's power pressing down upon him. The fate of the world hung in the balance as the group fought to prevent the sorcerer's resurgence.

With a final, resolute effort, Samuel secured the "Crown of Eclipse," the sorcerer's spectral form dissipating into the shadows.

With the "Crown of Eclipse" in their possession, the group emerged from the Great Pyramid, their mission fulfilled but at a great cost. The sorcerer's influence had been vanquished, but not without sacrifice.

Seraphina, weakened from the battle, knew that the artifacts must be safeguarded to prevent their dark power from being harnessed. With a heavy heart, she made a solemn decision.

"I will become the guardian of these artifacts," Seraphina declared. "I will ensure that they never fall into the wrong hands, and their power remains contained."

The Carrington family, though reluctant, understood the necessity of Seraphina's sacrifice. They bid her farewell, knowing that her destiny was intertwined with the artifacts and the legacy of the sorcerer.

As they left Cairo and returned to Ravenwood Manor, a sense of closure and triumph filled the air. The sorcerer's legacy had been thwarted, and the world was safe from the darkness that had threatened to consume it.

The Carrington family knew that their journey had been a harrowing one, filled with danger and sacrifice, but it had also been a testament to the power of unity and determination. The sorcerer's shadow had been dispelled, and the world could now embrace the light once more.

And so, the tale of the Carrington's and their battle against the sorcerer came to a close, a story of courage, sacrifice, and the triumph of good over darkness.

With Seraphina as the guardian of the artifacts, the Carrington family returned to Ravenwood Manor, their mission complete. The artifacts, each containing a piece of the sorcerer's soul, were safely secured within the hidden chamber.

As they gathered around the chamber, they reflected on the journey they had undertaken—the trials, the battles, and the sacrifices made to protect the world from the sorcerer's darkness.

Lady Eleanor spoke with pride in her voice. "Our family has faced the darkest of evils and emerged victorious. We have proven that the power of love, unity, and the determination to do what is right can overcome even the most of forces."

Samuel nodded in agreement.

"Our legacy is not one of darkness but of resilience and hope. We will ensure that the artifacts remain safeguarded, their power contained for all time."

With the sorcerer's influence vanquished, the Carrington family embraced a future filled with promise and light. They continued their legacy of philanthropy and goodwill, using their wealth and influence to make the world a better place.

Ravenwood Manor became a symbol of hope and sanctuary, a place where those in need could find solace and support. The Carrington's dedicated themselves to ensuring that the darkness they had faced would never again threaten the world.

As the years passed, the tale of their battle against the sorcerer became a legend—a story told to inspire future generations to stand against the forces of darkness and to protect the light within.

Seraphina, as the guardian of the artifacts, dedicated her life to their safekeeping. She studied their secrets and sought to understand the depths of the darkness they contained. Her knowledge became a beacon of wisdom for those who sought to harness magic for good.

Under Seraphina's watchful eye, the artifacts remained dormant, their power contained. She knew that the battle against darkness was ongoing, and her role as guardian was a solemn duty she would carry with honour.

The Carrington family's legacy was one of light and hope. Their tale served as a reminder that even in the face of the darkest of evils, the power of love, unity, and determination could prevail.

And so, the story of the Carrington's and their battle against the sorcerer came to an end, but their legacy endured—a legacy of resilience, courage, and the triumph of good over darkness.

The world was forever changed by their actions, and the shadows that had threatened to consume it had been dispelled.

In their wake, a brighter future awaited, where the light of hope would shine eternally. Years passed, and the world continued to thrive under the watchful gaze of the Carrington family and Seraphina. The artifacts remained safely guarded within Ravenwood Manor, their power contained. But as the world moved forward, a new chapter in their story was about to unfold.

One evening, as the sun set over the horizon, casting long shadows across the peaceful grounds of Ravenwood Manor, a mysterious visitor arrived at the manor's imposing gates. The visitor's identity was shrouded in secrecy, and their purpose remained unknown.

The visitor, cloaked in a hooded robe, approached the gates with an air of determination. They carried with them a sense of purpose that sent a shiver down the spine of the manor's caretaker, who had been faithfully tending to the estate for years.

The mysterious visitor was granted entry into Ravenwood Manor, and they were led to a dimly lit room where the Carrington family and Seraphina awaited. The room was adorned with ancient artifacts and relics, a testament to the family's history and their battle against the sorcerer.

With a voice masked by the hood of their robe, the visitor spoke in cryptic riddles and enigmatic phrases. They made a request that sent a ripple of unease through the room—a request to access the hidden chamber where the artifacts were safeguarded.

The Carrington family and Seraphina exchanged wary glances, their expressions reflecting the gravity of the situation. They knew all too well the importance of safeguarding the artifacts and preventing their formidable power from falling into the wrong hands. The visitor's true intentions remained shrouded in mystery, and trust was not something to be given lightly, especially when the fate of the world hung in the balance.

As they deliberated their next course of action, tension hung heavy in the air, each member of the group acutely aware of the weight of their decision. Lady Eleanor, her eyes narrowed in suspicion, voiced her concerns.

"We cannot afford to take any risks," she cautioned, her voice laced with determination. "The artifacts are too powerful to be entrusted to just anyone."

Sir Robert, ever the stalwart defender of their cause, nodded in agreement.

"Agreed," he affirmed, his tone resolute. "We must proceed with caution and ensure that the artifacts remain under our watchful eye at all times."

Professor Sinclair, the scholarly guardian of ancient knowledge, stroked his beard thoughtfully as he considered their options.

"While I understand the need for caution," he began, his voice measured, "we must also acknowledge the potential benefits of cooperation. If this visitor truly seeks to aid us in our quest, their assistance could prove invaluable."

Seraphina, her gaze steady and unwavering, weighed their words carefully before offering her own perspective.

"We cannot ignore the possibility that this visitor may hold the key to unlocking the mysteries surrounding the artifacts," she reasoned, her voice tinged with caution. "But we must proceed with caution and vigilance, ensuring that their true intentions align with our own."

After much deliberation and soul-searching, the Carrington family and Seraphina reached a decision. Though fraught with uncertainty, they agreed to grant the visitor's request, albeit under strict supervision.

"We will allow you access to the artifacts," Lady Eleanor declared, her tone firm, "but know that we will be watching closely. Any misstep, and you will answer to us."

With their decision made, the group prepared to face whatever challenges lay ahead, knowing that the fate of the world rested in their hands. For in the battle against darkness, trust was a rare commodity, and they would do whatever it took to ensure that their mission succeeded.

As the chamber's doors swung open, a wave of energy emanated from within, a reminder of the darkness contained within the artifacts. The visitor approached the artifacts with reverence, their hands trembling as they reached out to touch them. With a carefully executed incantation, the visitor began to unveil the true purpose of their visit. Shadows danced around them, and the artifacts responded, resonating with the visitor's presence.

The room filled with an eerie glow as the artifacts revealed their secrets. The sorcerer's plan had been more sinister than anyone had realised. It wasn't just a quest for power; it was a desperate attempt to undo a curse that had bound his soul to darkness for centuries.

The visitor, who had concealed their true identity beneath the shadowy depths of a hooded robe, stepped forward into the dim light of the chamber. With a deliberate motion, they cast aside the concealing garment, revealing themselves to be a descendant of the sorcerer—a descendant who bore the weight of their family's dark legacy and sought redemption from the curse that had plagued them for generations.

"I am of the bloodline of the sorcerer," the visitor declared, their voice carrying a solemn weight. "But I come not as an enemy, but as a seeker of truth and redemption. The curse that has haunted my family for centuries must be broken, and I believe that the artifacts you possess hold the key to our salvation."

Their words hung heavy in the air, fraught with the weight of centuries-old sorrow and desperation. The Carrington family and Seraphina exchanged wary glances, their expressions a mix of curiosity and apprehension. Could this descendant of the sorcerer be trusted, or were they merely another pawn in the game of darkness that threatened to consume them all?

As they pondered their next course of action, the visitor's gaze remained steady, unwavering in its resolve.

"I seek your aid in breaking the curse that has plagued my family for far too long," they continued, their voice tinged with urgency. "Together, we can unravel the mysteries of the past and forge a new future—one free from the shackles of darkness."

Their words resonated with the group, stirring something deep within their hearts. Despite the uncertainty that lingered in the air, there was a glimmer of hope—a belief that perhaps, just perhaps, redemption was possible, even in the darkest of times.

With a shared nod of agreement, the Carrington family and Seraphina extended their hands in a gesture of solidarity.

"We will aid you in your quest," Lady Eleanor vowed, her voice ringing with conviction. "But know this—we will not be deceived. The path to redemption is fraught with peril, and we will tread it with caution and vigilance."

And so, with their alliance forged and their purpose clear, the group prepared to embark on a journey that would test their resolve, their courage, and their faith in the face of unimaginable darkness. But as they stood united against the shadows that threatened to engulf them, they knew that together, they would prevail. For in the battle against the forces of evil, hope was the most powerful weapon of all.

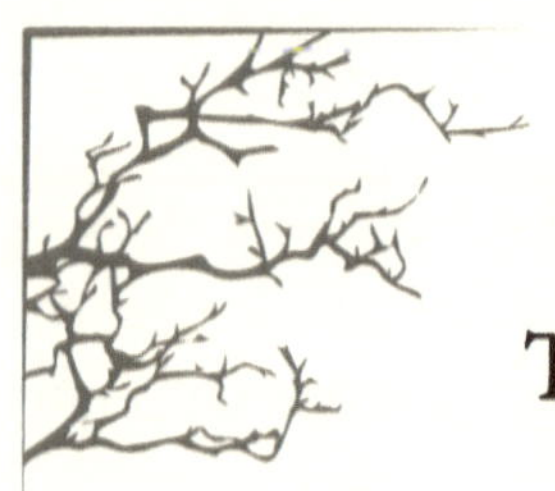

THE WITCH'S ASCENSION

The night had fallen like a heavy cloak over the sprawling estate of the Carrington family. The moon hung low in the ink-black sky, casting eerie shadows that seemed to dance with malice. Inside Ravenwood Manor, the once-forgotten chambers had come to life with an ominous purpose.

Within the hidden chamber, the artifacts lay dormant, their power contained. But a disturbance had awakened them, a presence that pulsed with dark energy. It was the malevolent sorcerer, his soul still fragmented but yearning for reunification.

As the sorcerer's influence grew, he reached out to the artifacts from the depths of his fragmented soul. His voice whispered through the corridors of Ravenwood Manor, a haunting melody of dark incantations and forbidden knowledge.

Deep within the manor, Samuel Carrington, the unwitting heir to the sorcerer's legacy, stirred in his sleep. He had grown up in the shadow of the artifacts, unaware of their true nature.

But now, as he slept, he felt a pull—an irresistible force drawing him toward the hidden chamber. In his dream, Samuel found himself standing at the threshold of the hidden chamber. The door swung open of its own accord, revealing the artifacts bathed in an eerie, light. They beckoned to him, their power radiating like a siren's call.

The sorcerer's voice echoed in Samuel's mind, filling his dreams with visions of power and darkness. He saw himself wielding the artifacts, commanding the forces of magic with an authority that transcended mortal understanding.

Samuel awoke with a start, his heart pounding with a mixture of fear and fascination. The dream had been vivid, too vivid to be dismissed as mere fantasy. He knew that the artifacts held a secret—a secret that he was destined to uncover.

Over the following days, Samuel's fascination with the artifacts grew. He began to spend more and more time in the hidden chamber, studying their intricate designs and deciphering the ancient runes etched upon them.

As he delved deeper into the artifacts' mysteries, Samuel's personality underwent a subtle transformation. He became more withdrawn, his thoughts consumed by the sorcerer's promises of power and ascension.

Lady Eleanor and Sir Robert noticed the change in their son's behaviour and grew increasingly concerned. They knew that the artifacts were not to be trifled with, that their power was a double-edged sword that could bring both enlightenment and damnation.

In the hushed silence of the chamber, Samuel's eyes narrowed as he approached the amulet, his senses alert to any sign of danger. The artifacts lay before him, their ancient power humming with an otherworldly energy that sent shivers down his spine.

As he reached out to grasp the amulet, a surge of dark energy coursed through him, sending tendrils of shadow dancing across his skin. Visions of twisted time and distorted reality flashed before his eyes, but he fought to maintain his grip on reality, his willpower bolstered by a newfound determination.

Whispers of ancient incantations echoed in his mind, beckoning him to unlock the secrets of the amulet and claim its power for his own.

"Embrace the darkness," the voices whispered, their words a seductive lure that promised untold power and dominion over all.

But Samuel hesitated, his mind wrestling with conflicting desires. On one hand, the allure of the amulet's power was undeniable, a temptation that threatened to consume him whole. Yet deep within his heart, a flicker of doubt remained—a glimmer of humanity that refused to be extinguished.

With a trembling hand, Samuel reached out once more, his fingers hovering inches above the pulsating surface of the amulet. The whispers grew louder, urging him to seize the power that lay within his grasp, to cast aside his doubts and embrace his destiny as the master of the arcane.

But just as he was on the verge of succumbing to the darkness, a single word echoed in his mind—a word spoken with a voice that echoed through the ages, a voice that carried the weight of centuries of struggle and sacrifice.

"Remember," the voice whispered, its timbre filled with an unmistakable sense of urgency. "Remember who you are, Samuel. Remember the light that still burns within you, even in the darkest of times."

The words struck a chord deep within Samuel's soul, stirring memories long buried beneath layers of pain and anger. Images flashed before his eyes—a loving family torn apart by tragedy, a young boy consumed by grief and loneliness, a journey of self-discovery fraught with peril and redemption.

With a sudden clarity, Samuel realised the truth that had been staring him in the face all along. The amulet was not the key to his salvation—it was a prison, a vessel of darkness that threatened to consume him if he allowed it to.

Drawing upon the strength of his newfound resolve, Samuel withdrew his hand from the amulet, his heart heavy with the weight of his decision.

"I will not be enslaved by darkness," he declared, his voice a defiant whisper against the shadows that sought to ensnare him.

And as he turned away from the amulet, leaving its dark power behind him, Samuel felt a glimmer of hope ignite within his heart—a hope that despite the trials and tribulations that lay ahead, he would never again lose sight of the light that still burned within him, guiding him on the path to redemption.

Samuel began to believe that he was destined for greatness, that he could harness the artifacts' power for the betterment of the world.

But Lady Eleanor and Sir Robert were not blind to their son's descent into darkness. They sought the guidance of Seraphina, the guardian of the artifacts, who had sensed the disturbance within the manor.

As the group gathered in the dimly lit chamber, Seraphina's voice rang out with a sense of urgency that cut through the tense silence like a knife.

"Listen to me," she began, her words carrying the weight of a warning too dire to ignore. "The sorcerer's resurgence is upon us, and his influence over Samuel grows stronger with each passing moment. We cannot afford to underestimate the threat he poses."

Her eyes blazed with determination as she addressed each member of the group in turn, her gaze unwavering as she imparted the gravity of their situation. "The sorcerer's soul is a malevolent force, one that seeks to reunite with Samuel and unleash untold chaos upon the world. We cannot allow that to happen."

Lady Eleanor nodded in solemn agreement, her expression a mirror of Seraphina's own resolve. "We have faced darkness before," she declared, her voice steady despite the weight of their predicament. "And we have emerged victorious. But this time, the stakes are higher than ever before."

Sir Robert, ever the stalwart defender of their cause, stepped forward, his features etched with determination. "We must act swiftly and decisively," he asserted, his voice carrying the authority of a leader born from years of battle. "The fate of the world hangs in the balance, and we are its last line of defence."

Professor Sinclair, the scholarly guardian of ancient knowledge, nodded in agreement, his expression grave. "We must find a way to thwart the sorcerer's plans and prevent his soul from reuniting with Samuel," he urged, his voice tinged with urgency. "But time is of the essence, and we cannot afford to hesitate."

With a shared nod of determination, the group resolved to face the looming threat head-on, their hearts united in a common purpose. For in the battle against darkness, they knew that unity was their greatest strength—a bond forged in the fires of adversity and tempered by the trials of their journey.

And as they prepared to confront the sorcerer's resurgence and safeguard the world from untold chaos, Seraphina's words echoed in their minds, a solemn reminder of the task that lay before them. "We must act swiftly," she reiterated, her voice a beacon of hope in the encroaching darkness. "For the fate of the world depends on it."

The Carrington family confronted Samuel, pleading with him to resist the sorcerer's influence. They spoke of the dangers of unchecked ambition and the price that would be paid for wielding the artifacts' power.

But Samuel, consumed by his newfound obsession, turned a deaf ear to them.

He believed that he alone could master the artifacts and bend their power to his will.

A battle raged within Samuel's soul, a battle between the light of his upbringing and the darkness that beckoned to him. The sorcerer's whispers grew louder, drowning out the voices of reason and love.

One fateful night, as a storm raged outside Ravenwood Manor, Samuel Carrington made his choice.

The incantation Samuel recited as he donned the artifacts was a powerful invocation, its words resonating with ancient magic and dark energy. With each syllable, the air crackled with tension, and the very fabric of reality seemed to warp and bend to his will.

The words he spoke were a testament to the depths of his newfound power, a dark symphony that echoed through the chamber with an eerie resonance. They were a potent blend of archaic language and forbidden knowledge, each phrase imbued with the essence of shadow and mystery.

"By shadows deep and darkness old, By moon and star, and secrets untold,

I call upon the ancient might, To cloak me now in veil of night.

With crown of eclipse upon my brow, Grant me power, here and now,

To wield the darkness, to bend the night, And bring all foes within my sight.

Scroll of shadows, reveal your lore, Unleash the magic that lies in store,

With whispered words of ancient tongue, Let darkness rise, and light be shunned.

Shroud of shadows, wrap me tight, Conceal my form from mortal sight,

In shadow's embrace, I shall reside, Master of darkness, with power to decide.

By this incantation, I command, Darkness obey, at my hand.

With artifacts three, I now decree, My will be done, so mote it be."

As Samuel's voice filled the air, the artifacts responded to his command, their surfaces shimmering with an otherworldly glow. The "Shroud of Shadows" wrapped around him like a cloak of darkness, concealing his form from prying eyes and granting him the ability to move unseen through the night.

The "Crown of Eclipse" settled upon his brow, its ancient runes pulsating with an ominous light. With its power coursing through him, Samuel felt a surge of dark energy flow through his veins, filling him with a sense of unstoppable might.

And finally, the "Scroll of Shadows" unfurled before him, its pages crackling with arcane energy. As Samuel traced his fingers along the ancient glyphs inscribed upon its surface, he felt a connection to the very essence of shadow itself, a power that promised dominion over all who dared oppose him.

With the artifacts in place and the incantation complete, Samuel stood poised on the brink of a new era—one where his dark ambitions would know no bounds. And as he gazed upon the world with eyes filled with malevolent intent, he knew that nothing could stand in his way. For he was Samuel Carrington, master of shadow and wielder of the darkest magic imaginable. And soon, all would bow before his might.

Dark energy surged through him, coursing like a torrent of malevolence. The artifacts responded to his command, their power amplifying his every desire.

Samuel's ascent to witch hood was complete. The sorcerer's soul fragments rejoined, their unity a testament to Samuel's newfound mastery over the artifacts.

With the artifacts at his command, Samuel's power knew no bounds. He unleashed dark spells and illusions that plunged Ravenwood Manor into an abyss of shadow and despair. The very walls of the manor seemed to tremble in fear as Samuel's energy surged.

Lady Eleanor and Sir Robert, along with Seraphina, confronted Samuel in a final, desperate effort to save their son from the darkness that had consumed him. But Samuel's power was too great, his ambition too relentless.

In a devastating display of power, Samuel turned his newfound abilities against his own family. Lady Eleanor and Sir Robert were rendered powerless before him, their pleas for mercy falling on deaf ears.

Samuel Carrington stood at the pinnacle of power, his once-human form now infused with the dark energies of witchcraft. With each passing day, his mastery over the arcane arts grew stronger, his influence spreading like wildfire across the globe.

From the shadows, Samuel watched as the world trembled at his feet, its leaders bowing before his might or facing the wrath of his dark magic. His ambitions knew no bounds, his hunger for power insatiable as he sought to bend reality itself to his will.

In the corridors of power, whispers of Samuel's dark deeds echoed, spreading fear and uncertainty among those who dared to oppose him. He had become a legend, a myth whispered in hushed tones by those who knew the true extent of his power.

But Samuel cared little for the opinions of mortals. To him, they were mere insects scurrying beneath his feet, their lives inconsequential in the face of his grand design for the world. And as he gazed out upon the chaos he had wrought, a twisted smile played upon his lips, a silent testament to his triumph over the forces of light and righteousness.

As Samuel's influence spread, fear gripped the hearts of all who dared to oppose him. Entire nations fell under his dark spell, their leaders trembling before his might. Those who resisted were swiftly dealt with, their defiance crushed beneath the weight of Samuel's relentless ambition.

In the shadows, Samuel became a spectral figure, a harbinger of doom whose very presence sent shivers down the spines of even the bravest souls. His dark powers knew no bounds, and he wielded them with a ruthlessness that left a trail of devastation in his wake.

But for Samuel, power was not merely a means to an end—it was an end in itself. With each victory, each conquest, he felt his grasp on reality tighten, his control over the world solidify. And as he looked out upon the chaos he had wrought, he revelled in the knowledge that he alone held the keys to the future of mankind.

Yet even as Samuel's dark reign spread like a cancer across the world, there were those who dared to defy him. Secret societies and underground movements rose up in rebellion, seeking to overthrow the tyrant who held the world in his iron grip.

But Samuel was no fool. He knew that his enemies lurked in the shadows, plotting his downfall. And with each passing day, he grew ever more vigilant, ever more determined to crush any who dared to challenge his authority.

For Samuel Carrington, the world was his playground, and he would stop at nothing to ensure that his reign of terror endured for all eternity.

Samuel Carrington's lust for power knew no bounds, and he delighted in the chaos and despair that he spread like a disease across the world. From his hidden lair, he manipulated reality itself, bending it to his will with a flick of his wrist and a whispered incantation.

Cities burned at his command, their once-proud streets reduced to smouldering ruins under the relentless assault of his dark magic. Governments toppled, their leaders powerless to resist the overwhelming might of Samuel's malevolence.

But amidst the devastation, a glimmer of hope still flickered in the hearts of the brave few who dared to defy him. Resistance movements sprang up like wildfire, their members united in their determination to overthrow the tyrant who held their world in thrall.

Yet Samuel was no stranger to adversity. With each threat to his power, he unleashed his dark forces with a ferocity that knew no bounds, crushing dissent with a merciless efficiency that sent a chill down the spine of even the most hardened rebel.

And as the world descended further into darkness, Samuel's grip on reality tightened, his influence spreading like a poison that seeped into every corner of the globe. Those who dared to oppose him were met with swift and brutal retribution, their hopes dashed against the rocks of Samuel's unyielding will.

But even as Samuel's power grew, so too did the whispers of dissent. In the darkest corners of the world, a resistance was building, its members drawn together by a shared determination to end Samuel's reign of terror once and for all. And as they prepared to strike, they knew that their struggle would be long and arduous, but they also knew that they fought for the very soul of humanity itself.

Samuel Carrington's reign of witchcraft brought about a world plunged into darkness, where fear and uncertainty reigned supreme. His manipulation of reality became the stuff of legend, as tales of his dark deeds spread far and wide, striking terror into the hearts of all who heard them.

Entire nations crumbled under the weight of Samuel's malevolent influence, their citizens enslaved by his dark magic and twisted visions of power. The once-vibrant cities lay in ruins, their streets haunted by the echoes of Samuel's laughter as he enjoyed his newfound dominion.

But amidst the chaos, there were those who dared to resist, who refused to bow before the tyrant who held their world in his iron grip. They banded together in secret, forming alliances and plotting rebellion against the dark forces that threatened to consume them all.

Yet Samuel was not content to merely hold sway over the physical realm. He sought to control the very fabric of reality itself, to bend it to his will and reshape it according to his own twisted desires. With each passing day, his powers grew stronger, his influence more pervasive.

And as the world teetered on the brink of oblivion, Samuel Carrington stood at its centre, a malevolent force of darkness whose ambition knew no bounds. He luxuriated in the chaos and destruction he had wrought, knowing that he alone held the keys to the world's salvation—or its ultimate demise.

Samuel Carrington's reign of witchcraft brought about a world plunged into darkness, where fear and uncertainty reigned supreme. His manipulation of reality became the stuff of legend, as tales of his dark deeds spread far and wide, striking terror into the hearts of all who heard them.

Entire nations crumbled under the weight of Samuel's malevolent influence, their citizens enslaved by his dark magic and twisted visions of power. The once-vibrant cities lay in ruins, their streets haunted by the echoes of Samuel's laughter as he took pleasure in his newfound dominion.

But amidst the chaos, there were those who dared to resist, who refused to bow before the tyrant who held their world in his iron grip. They banded together in secret, forming alliances and plotting rebellion against the dark forces that threatened to consume them all.

Yet Samuel was not content to merely hold sway over the physical realm. He sought to control the very fabric of reality itself, to bend it to his will and reshape it according to his own twisted desires. With each passing day, his powers grew stronger, his influence more pervasive.

And as the world teetered on the brink of oblivion, Samuel Carrington stood at its centre, a malevolent force of darkness whose ambition knew no bounds. He savoured the chaos and destruction he had wrought, knowing that he alone held the keys to the world's salvation—or its ultimate demise.

In the darkest depths of Samuel Carrington's twisted mind, a sense of triumph welled up as he surveyed the world he had brought to its knees. The once-thriving civilisations lay in ruins, their people cowering in fear at the mere mention of his name.

Yet, amidst the devastation, there flickered a faint glimmer of hope—a spark of resistance that refused to be extinguished. The brave souls who dared to stand against Samuel's tyranny rallied together, drawing strength from each other as they prepared to face the ultimate battle for freedom.

But Samuel Carrington was not about to relinquish his grip on power so easily. With every fibre of his being, he poured his dark energy into maintaining his stranglehold on reality, his malevolent laughter echoing through the desolate wasteland he had created.

As the forces of light and darkness clashed in a final, cataclysmic showdown, the fate of the world hung in the balance. The outcome of the battle would determine the course of history, shaping the destiny of mankind for generations to come.

And as Samuel Carrington stood on the precipice of victory, a twisted smile played upon his lips, his eyes alight with the fires of madness. For he knew that, in the end, it was not the strength of arms or the power of magic that would decide the victor, but the resilience of the human spirit and the unyielding determination of those who refused to surrender to the darkness.

People lived in constant fear, their lives subject to Samuel's whims. His spells brought forth nightmares, twisted illusions, and a sense of hopelessness that hung like a suffocating shroud.

The Carrington family, devastated by Samuel's fall from grace, became fugitives in a world ruled by their own flesh and blood. Lady Eleanor and Sir Robert had not given up hope; they believed that there must be a way to break the sorcerer's hold over their son.

In the darkest corner of the world, the Carrington's sought guidance from Seraphina, the guardian of the artifacts. She spoke of an ancient prophecy, a prophecy that foretold of a chosen one who would rise to challenge the witch's reign.

"The sorcerer's power is great," Seraphina explained, "but it is not without its weaknesses. The artifacts that granted him his power can also be used against him, but only by one with a pure heart and unwavering determination."

The Carrington's knew that the prophecy held the key to their son's redemption and the salvation of the world. They embarked on a quest to gather the knowledge and allies needed to fulfil the prophecy and bring an end to Samuel's reign of terror.

The Carrington's' quest led them to the far reaches of the world, where they sought out ancient wisdom and allies who could aid them

In their battle against Samuel. They encountered mystics, warriors, and scholars who had long guarded the secrets of the sorcerer.

Each ally they gathered possessed unique knowledge and abilities that would prove invaluable in the impending showdown. They learned of rituals, incantations, and spells that could weaken Samuel's power and break the artifacts' hold over him.

The chosen one of the prophecy remained a mystery, but the Carrington's believed that their journey would ultimately lead them to the one who could challenge Samuel's malevolence.

With their allies and newfound knowledge in tow, the Carrington family returned to Ravenwood Manor, where they would face Samuel in a final, cataclysmic showdown.

The battlefield crackled with energy as Samuel Carrington, now a formidable witch of immense power, faced off against the combined forces of light and goodness. His dark aura radiated malevolence, casting shadows that seemed to swallow the very essence of hope.

The Carringtons, their resolve steeled by the love they bore for each other and their world, stood at the forefront of the battle. Lady Eleanor's eyes blazed with determination as she brandished her sword, while Sir Robert's hands crackled with arcane energy, ready to unleash his magic upon their foe.

Seraphina, her voice ringing out like a clarion call, chanted ancient incantations that wove a protective barrier around their allies. Her words echoed across the battlefield, a beacon of hope amidst the encroaching darkness.

But Samuel was not alone in his quest for domination. He was bolstered by a legion of dark creatures—twisted beings born of his own malevolent magic. They swarmed around him like a swarm of angry hornets, their eyes gleaming with hunger as they lunged at their prey.

As the two sides clashed, the air crackled with the clash of steel and the roar of magic. Spells flew like arrows, striking down friend and foe alike with deadly precision. The ground shook with the force of their battle, the very earth trembling beneath their feet.

But amidst the chaos, the Carringtons and their allies fought on, their determination unshaken by the ferocity of their enemy. For they knew that they fought not just for themselves, but for the very soul of their world—a world that stood on the brink of annihilation at the hands of Samuel Carrington and his dark forces.

The clash between light and darkness intensified as Samuel Carrington unleashed a barrage of dark magic upon his adversaries. Shadows danced across the battlefield, twisting and writhing as they sought to engulf their foes in an inescapable abyss.

But the Carringtons and their allies were not so easily vanquished. With every strike, they pushed back against the encroaching darkness, their weapons flashing like beacons of hope amidst the gloom. Lady Eleanor's sword sliced through the air with deadly precision, while Sir Robert's spells crackled with raw power, striking down their enemies with righteous fury.

Seraphina's incantations grew in strength and intensity, weaving a protective barrier around their allies that shimmered with radiant light. Her voice echoed across the battlefield, a beacon of hope amidst the encroaching darkness.

Yet, for every blow they landed, Samuel seemed to grow stronger, his dark energy pulsing with malevolent power. His laughter echoed across the battlefield, a chilling reminder of the horrors that awaited should he emerge victorious.

But the Carringtons and their allies refused to yield. With every ounce of their strength, they pushed back against the tide of darkness, their determination unyielding in the face of overwhelming odds.

For they knew that the fate of their world hung in the balance, and they would not rest until they had vanquished the darkness that threatened to consume them all.

As the battle raged on, the very fabric of reality seemed to tremble under the weight of Samuel's dark magic. The ground beneath their feet quaked with the force of his power, and the air crackled with the energy of their conflict.

The Carringtons and their allies fought with a ferocity born of desperation, their every movement a testament to their determination to emerge victorious. Lady Eleanor's sword flashed in the darkness, cutting through the shadows with uncanny precision, while Sir Robert's spells danced through the air like bolts of lightning, striking down their enemies with deadly accuracy.

Seraphina's incantations filled the air with a melodic cadence, weaving a protective barrier around their allies that shimmered with radiant light. Her voice rang out like a clarion call, rallying their forces and bolstering their resolve in the face of overwhelming odds.

But Samuel was not about to be defeated so easily. With a wave of his hand, he unleashed a wave of dark energy that engulfed their allies in a maelstrom of shadows. The Carringtons and their allies fought valiantly against the onslaught, but it seemed as though their efforts were in vain.

Yet even in the darkest hour, hope remained. For as long as the Carringtons and their allies stood together, there was still a chance—a chance to push back against the darkness and reclaim their world from the clutches of evil.

In the midst of the chaos, Samuel's laughter echoed through the air like a chilling refrain, his voice filled with malice and triumph. He took pleasure in the destruction he wrought, relishing the fear and despair that gripped his enemies' hearts.

But the Carringtons and their allies refused to surrender to despair. With renewed determination, they pushed back against the tide of darkness, their weapons flashing with a newfound resolve.

Lady Eleanor's sword blazed with righteous fury as she struck down Samuel's minions with unmatched skill and precision. Sir Robert's spells crackled with raw power, driving back the dark forces that sought to overwhelm them.

Seraphina's incantations wove a protective barrier around their allies, shielding them from the worst of Samuel's assaults. Her voice rang out with unwavering resolve, a beacon of hope amidst the encroaching darkness.

As the battle raged on, the lines between friend and foe blurred, and alliances shifted like sand in the wind. But through it all, one thing remained constant—the unwavering resolve of the Carringtons and their allies to stand against the darkness and fight for the future of their world.

The artifacts, once instruments of malevolence, now served as a beacon of redemption. They channelled the combined strength of the Carrington family and their allies, their power amplified by the purity of their hearts.

In a climactic moment of reckoning, the sorcerer's hold over Samuel began to weaken. The artifacts, drained of their dark power, could no longer sustain his ascent.

Samuel, his eyes filled with a mixture of fear and regret, began to realise the depths of his descent into darkness. He struggled against the sorcerer's influence, clawing his way back to the light.

In an act of ultimate sacrifice, Lady Eleanor and Sir Robert used their own magic to weaken the sorcerer's hold over their son. With their powers combined, they created a protective barrier that allowed Samuel to break free from the sorcerer's grasp.

As the sorcerer's influence faded, Samuel Carrington returned to himself, his heart filled with remorse for the atrocities he had committed. He had seen the true nature of power, the devastation it could bring, and the darkness it could unleash.

With the artifacts drained of their energy, the Carrington's and their allies sealed them away once more, deep within the hidden chamber. Samuel vowed to dedicate his life to making amends for the suffering he had caused and to ensure that the artifacts would never again fall into the wrong hands.

The world slowly began to heal from the wounds inflicted by Samuel's reign of witchcraft. The Carrington family, with their allies, worked tirelessly to rebuild and restore hope to a world that had been plunged into darkness.

Ravenwood Manor became a sanctuary once more, a place of solace and support for those in need. The Carrington's' legacy was one of redemption and resilience, a testament to the power of love and unity to overcome even the darkest of evils.

Samuel, forever changed by his journey from darkness to redemption, dedicated himself to the study of magic and the protection of the artifacts. He became a guardian of ancient knowledge, vowing to use his abilities for the betterment of the world.

Lady Eleanor and Sir Robert, proud of their son's transformation, continued their philanthropic endeavours, spreading light and hope to those in need. Seraphina, the guardian of the artifacts, remained a steadfast ally, her wisdom and guidance a source of strength for the Carrington family.

In the wake of the sorcerer's defeat, the prophecy of redemption had been fulfilled. The chosen one, whose heart had remained pure and unwavering, had emerged from the shadows.

The chosen one was not a single individual but a symbol of the collective strength and determination of those who had stood against the darkness. It was a reminder that, even in the face of overwhelming evil, the power of unity and love could prevail.

The world had been forever changed by the events that had unfolded within Ravenwood Manor, but it had emerged stronger and more resilient than ever before.

As time passed, the story of the Carrington family's battle against the sorcerer became a legend—a tale of redemption, sacrifice, and the triumph of good over darkness. It served as a beacon of hope for future generations, a reminder that no matter how far one may fall, there is always a path back to the light.

Ravenwood Manor stood as a symbol of that legacy, a place where the darkness of the past had been banished, and the light of hope shone eternally.

And so, the tale of the Carrington's and their battle against the sorcerer came to an end, but their legacy endured—a legacy of resilience, courage, and the unwavering belief that even in the darkest of times, the power of love and unity would always prevail.

A WEB OF DECEIT

Years had passed since Ds Karl Cushnahan had last set foot in Ravenwood Manor. He had become a seasoned detective, known for his tenacity and unwavering pursuit of justice.

But the case of Father Thomas's murder had never left his mind, and it continued to gnaw at him like an unsolved puzzle.

One day, as he was going through old case files, a newfound determination washed over him. He had vowed to find the priest's killer, and he realised that he could not let the mystery remain unsolved any longer. With renewed resolve, he decided to revisit Ravenwood Manor, where it had all begun.

As he stepped through the imposing front doors of the manor, memories of his previous visit flooded back. The sense of foreboding and the secrets that lurked within its walls had not diminished with time. He knew that he was playing with fire, for the forces that had once consumed Samuel Carrington could still linger.

Meanwhile, within the depths of Ravenwood Manor, Samuel Carrington had managed to keep his witch hood at bay. Years of self-reflection and dedication to the study of magic had allowed him to control the darkness that had once consumed him. He had become a guardian of the artifacts, ensuring that their malevolent power remained sealed away. But Samuel's newfound peace was shattered when he learned of Ds Cushnahan's return. The detective's relentless pursuit had not gone unnoticed, and Samuel knew that his secrets were in danger of being exposed.

As Ds Cushnahan delved deeper into the mysteries of Ravenwood Manor, he found himself unravelling a complex tapestry of secrets and lies that had been carefully woven over centuries. Each room he explored held its own secrets, each corridor whispered of untold horrors hidden in the shadows.

In the archives of the manor, he discovered ancient manuscripts and dusty tomes that spoke of dark rituals and forbidden knowledge. The pages were filled with cryptic symbols and arcane incantations, hinting at powers beyond mortal comprehension.

But it was not just the written word that held clues to the manor's dark past. As he searched the sprawling estate, Cushnahan stumbled upon hidden passageways and secret chambers, each one a testament to the depths of depravity that had taken root within these walls.

In one particularly secluded chamber, he found a series of ornate tapestries that depicted scenes of unspeakable horror—sacrifices made in the name of dark gods, rituals performed to summon malevolent spirits from the depths of the underworld.

But perhaps the most chilling discovery of all was the revelation of the manor's true purpose. Beneath its grand façade lay a labyrinth of tunnels and catacombs, a network of hidden passages that stretched deep beneath the earth. Here, in the heart of Ravenwood Manor, lay the source of its power—a source that had been carefully guarded for generations, its secrets known only to a select few.

As Cushnahan pieced together the fragments of the manor's dark history, he realised that he had stumbled upon something far more sinister than he could have ever imagined. The web of deceit he had uncovered stretched back centuries, its tendrils reaching out to ensnare all who dared to uncover its secrets. And at its centre, lurking in the shadows, was the true mastermind behind it all—a figure whose dark influence had shaped the fate of Ravenwood Manor for generations.

As Ds Cushnahan delved deeper into the investigation, he found himself face to face with the remaining members of the Carrington family, including Samuel, who now presented himself as a reformed man. The atmosphere in the room was tense, each member of the family eyeing Cushnahan with a mixture of suspicion and apprehension.

Cushnahan began his questioning, his voice steady but firm as he sought to unravel the truth hidden beneath the surface.

"Mr. Carrington," he began, addressing Samuel directly, "I understand that you've had quite the transformation in recent years. Care to tell me about it?"

Samuel's expression was guarded, his eyes betraying a hint of uncertainty as he responded.

"Yes, well, it's been a journey, to say the least," he replied, his tone carefully measured. "I've made mistakes in the past, but I've worked hard to atone for them. I'm a different man now, Detective, I assure you."

Cushnahan studied Samuel carefully, noting the subtle shifts in his demeanour as he spoke. There was something in the way he held himself, a sense of unease that seemed to linger just beneath the surface.

"And what about your family?" Cushnahan pressed, turning his attention to the others in the room. "Do they share your sentiments?"

Lady Eleanor and Sir Robert exchanged a hesitant glance, their expressions betraying a hint of doubt.

"We want to believe that Samuel has changed," Lady Eleanor began, her voice tinged with uncertainty, "but there have been...incidents that give us cause for concern."

Cushnahan's interest was piqued.

"Incidents?" he prompted, leaning forward slightly in his chair. "What sort of incidents?"

Sir Robert hesitated for a moment before speaking, his voice low and measured.

"Strange occurrences, Detective," he replied cryptically. "Unexplained phenomena that seem to follow Samuel wherever he goes. We've tried to ignore them, but they've only grown more frequent in recent weeks."

Cushnahan's brow furrowed in concern as he listened to their accounts. It was clear that there was more to Samuel's transformation than met the eye, and he vowed to get to the bottom of it, no matter the cost.

Ds Cushnahan's presence became a constant source of tension within Ravenwood Manor. Samuel knew that the detective's probing questions could lead to the unravelling of his carefully constructed facade. He had to tread carefully, for at any moment, he could revert back to his old ways and seek to eliminate the nosy policeman.

The detective's investigation led him to the hidden chamber within the manor, where the artifacts had once held their power. As he stood before the sealed door, he felt a sense of unease wash over him. He knew that the answers to Father Thomas's murder and the mysteries of Ravenwood Manor lay within.

Unbeknownst to Ds Cushnahan, Samuel watched from the shadows, his eyes filled with a mixture of fear and determination. He knew that the detective was on the brink of discovering the truth, and he would stop at nothing to protect his secrets.

As the web of deceit continued to unravel, the fate of Ravenwood Manor hung in the balance. Ds Karl Cushnahan played a dangerous game of cat and mouse with Samuel Carrington, unaware that the forces he sought to uncover were ready to strike back with a vengeance. The battle of wits had begun, and the stakes had never been higher.

As Ds Cushnahan retreated from Ravenwood Manor, Samuel Carrington wasted no time. He knew that his secrets were at risk of being exposed, and he couldn't allow that to happen.

Returning to the hidden chamber, Samuel faced the sealed door with a determined glint in his eye. He entered and reached out to the artifacts, his fingers trembling as he broke the seals that had held their power at bay.

The moment the artifacts were unsealed, a surge of dark energy washed over Samuel. It was a sensation he had not felt in years—the rush of power, the intoxicating allure of malevolence.

He welcomed it with open arms, for he knew that it was the key to his survival. With newfound power coursing through his veins, Samuel set his sights on Ds Cushnahan. He began to plague the detective with night terrors, vivid and horrifying dreams that left him sleepless and haunted. Strange occurrences unfolded around him, objects moving of their own accord, whispers in the darkness, and eerie shadows that seemed to follow his every step.

Ds Cushnahan's resolve wavered as he grappled with the relentless onslaught of the supernatural. He couldn't explain the inexplicable, and a growing sense of unease settled over him.

He knew that he was being pushed to the brink, and Samuel Carrington's intentions were clear. Ds Cushnahan refused to back down. He had faced darkness before, and he was not about to let fear consume him. He delved deeper into the mysteries of Ravenwood Manor, seeking allies who could help him combat the evil forces at play.

But Samuel Carrington was relentless in his pursuit of vengeance. He used the artifacts to manipulate reality, to blur the lines between dreams and waking life. The detective's nights became a battleground, where he fought against the onslaught with sheer determination.

As the battle of wills raged on, the stakes grew higher. Ds Cushnahan knew that he was inching closer to the truth, but he was also perilously close to the brink of madness. Samuel Carrington's power threatened to consume him, and the detective's grip on reality began to slip.

In a moment of desperation, Ds Cushnahan revisited Samuel Carrington, hoping to reason with the man he believed to be the key to unravelling the mysteries of Ravenwood Manor.

"I know what you're doing," Ds Cushnahan said, his voice steady despite the turmoil within him. "I won't be deterred by your tricks and illusions. I will uncover the truth, no matter the cost." Samuel met his gaze, a sinister smile playing on his lips.

"Detective, you underestimate the power I possess. If you wish to enter that chamber and learn the secrets it holds, you will need more than determination. You will need a search warrant."

Ds Cushnahan left Ravenwood Manor once more, his resolve unshaken but his frustration mounting. Samuel Carrington's resurgence had pushed him to the edge, and he knew that the battle was far from over.

As he stepped out into the darkness, Ds Cushnahan vowed to return with the necessary warrant. He would not rest until he uncovered the truth behind Father Thomas's murder and put an end to the forces that plagued Ravenwood Manor. But little did he know that Samuel Carrington had no intention of relinquishing his secrets, and the battle between light and darkness was far from its conclusion.

MANIPULATION AND BETRAYAL

Within the confines of Ravenwood Manor, Samuel Carrington's power continued to grow. The artifacts, unsealed and under his control, imbued him with a dark energy that knew no bounds. His desire for power and vengeance had become an insatiable hunger.

One day, Samuel's parents, Lord and Lady Carrington, decided to pay their son a visit. They had heard rumours of their son's transformation and the troubling events surrounding the manor. Concerned for his well-being, they hoped to intervene and bring him back to the path of light.

As they arrived at the imposing gates of Ravenwood Manor, Samuel watched them from an upper window, his eyes filled with a gleam. He had no intention of letting anyone interfere with his plans, not even his own parents.

As Lord and Lady Carrington drove up the winding road that led to the manor, their hearts pounded with anticipation, their minds filled with thoughts of the family reunion that awaited them. But as they approached the imposing gates of Ravenwood Manor, their excitement turned to apprehension, a sense of unease settling over them like a shroud.

Suddenly, without warning, their car lurched forward, its engine roaring to life with a deafening roar. Lord Carrington's hands tightened on the steering wheel, his knuckles turning white with fear as he struggled to regain control. But no matter how hard he tried, the car seemed to have a mind of its own, hurtling forward at a dangerous speed.

Beside him, Lady Carrington's screams filled the air, her voice raw with terror as she clung to her seat, her eyes wide with fear.

"Richard, what's happening?" she cried, her voice trembling with fear. "We need to stop the car!"

But try as they might, their efforts were in vain. The car continued to accelerate, its speed increasing with each passing second. The wind whipped through the open windows, tearing at their clothes and hair as they hurtled towards the looming gates of the manor.

In that moment, terror consumed them, their minds racing with thoughts of impending doom. What unseen force was behind this madness? What dark power had taken hold of their car and sent them hurtling towards their own demise?

As they approached the gates, their fate seemed inevitable. And then, with a sickening crunch, their car collided with a tree, the impact sending flames erupting around them. The intense heat seared their skin, the flames engulfing them in a fiery inferno.

Their screams echoed through the night, a haunting chorus of agony and despair as they were consumed by the flames. In that moment of horror, their lives were snuffed out, their bodies reduced to nothing but ash and smoke.

As the flames finally died down and the smoke cleared, all that remained was the charred wreckage of their car, a grim reminder of the tragedy that had unfolded. And in the darkness of the night, Samuel's laughter rang out, a chilling echo of the evil that had claimed their lives. He had seen their attempt to intervene as an act of betrayal, a threat to his newfound power, and he had no qualms about eliminating them to protect his secrets.

With Lord and Lady Carrington's deaths, Samuel felt a surge of malevolence that coursed through his veins. He had crossed a line from which there was no turning back. His descent into darkness was now complete, and he would stop at nothing to achieve his ultimate goal—to amass power beyond imagination and unleash a reign of terror that would rival even the darkest of sorcerers.

As the flames of his parents' car illuminated the night, Samuel Carrington's malevolent laughter echoed through Ravenwood Manor. He knew that he would not be stopped, that the forces of light and justice were no match for the wickedness that now resided within him. The battle had taken a sinister turn, and manipulation and betrayal had become his most potent weapons in the pursuit of his insidious agenda.

As the flames of the burning car illuminated the night sky, a chorus of sirens wailed in the distance. The sound of approaching police cars and fire engines echoed through the once-quiet grounds of Ravenwood Manor. Samuel Carrington watched with a sense of triumph, believing that he had successfully eliminated any threats to his ambitions.

The police and fire services arrived at the scene with a sense of urgency, their flashing lights casting an eerie glow on the smouldering wreckage of Lord and Lady Carrington's car. Firefighters worked tirelessly to extinguish the flames, their efforts in vain as the vehicle was reduced to a charred, twisted mass of metal.

Ds Karl Cushnahan arrived shortly after, his heart heavy with a sense of foreboding. He knew that the circumstances surrounding the crash were suspicious, and he couldn't shake the feeling that Samuel Carrington was somehow involved.

Approaching the scene, Ds Cushnahan quickly assessed the situation. He spoke with the firefighters and examined the car, searching for any evidence of foul play. But the fire chief, a seasoned veteran, shook his head and addressed the detective.

"Nothing here indicates arson or any suspicious circumstances, Detective Cushnahan," the fire chief explained. "It appears that the accelerator was stuck on, causing the crash and subsequent fire. There's no sign of foul play."

Ds Cushnahan felt frustration welling up within him. The evidence he needed to link Samuel Carrington to the tragedy remained elusive, and without it, obtaining a search warrant for Ravenwood Manor would be nearly impossible.

Meanwhile, Samuel Carrington stood at the outskirts of the scene, his expression one of feigned shock and grief. He knew that his actions had to appear genuine, and he played the part of the bereaved son to perfection.

As Ds Cushnahan approached Samuel, he offered his condolences, his voice filled with sympathy.

"I'm truly sorry for your loss, Mr Carrington. We'll conduct a thorough investigation to determine the cause of the accident."

Samuel nodded; his eyes filled with tears that were as false as his remorse.

"Thank you, Detective. This is a tragedy beyond words. I never expected anything like this to happen."

Ds Cushnahan scrutinised Samuel carefully, searching for any hint of guilt or deception. But Samuel's facade was flawless, his grief convincing.

As the fire chief continued to explain the circumstances to Ds Cushnahan, the detective couldn't help but feel trapped. He knew that Samuel Carrington was responsible for the crash, but without concrete evidence, he had no legal basis to obtain a search warrant for Ravenwood Manor.

With a heavy heart and a gnawing sense of defeat, Ds Cushnahan left the scene, vowing to continue his quest for evidence.

He couldn't allow Samuel to escape justice, and he knew that the sorcerer's power had grown stronger with each passing day.

The battle between light and darkness had taken a sinister turn, and Samuel Carrington's calculated facade had kept him one step ahead of the law. Ds Karl Cushnahan was determined to uncover the truth, but he also knew that he was running out of time. Samuel's power threatened to consume everything in its path, and the detective's desperate quest for evidence had become a race against the forces of darkness.

Ds Karl Cushnahan left the scene of the tragic car crash, frustration weighing heavily on his shoulders. He was determined to uncover the truth about Samuel Carrington's involvement in the accident and his connection to the mysteries of Ravenwood Manor, but the evidence remained elusive.

As he walked away from the scene, deep in thought, Ds Cushnahan came across a small roadside cafe. It was a quaint, dimly lit place, with an air of mystery that seemed to beckon to him. He decided to stop for a moment, to clear his mind and gather his thoughts.

Sitting at the counter, he ordered a cup of coffee and watched as the rain began to fall outside. The cafe was nearly empty, save for a few patrons scattered about. One of them, a middle-aged woman with a weathered look, caught his eye.

She sat alone at a corner table, sipping her tea and seemingly lost in thought. Something about her demeanour struck Ds Cushnahan as unusual, as if she carried a weight of knowledge that went beyond her years.

As he sipped his coffee, Ds Cushnahan couldn't help but feel drawn to the woman. He decided to strike up a conversation, hoping that she might hold the key to unravelling the mysteries that surrounded Samuel Carrington and Ravenwood Manor.

Approaching her table, he offered a polite smile.

"Mind if I join you for a moment? I couldn't help but notice that you seem like someone who might have a story to tell."

The woman looked up, her eyes filled with a mixture of surprise and curiosity. She studied Ds Cushnahan for a moment before nodding, inviting him to take a seat.

"You have a keen intuition, Detective. I do indeed have a story, one that is intertwined with the secrets of Ravenwood Manor."

Ds Cushnahan's heart quickened. Could this chance encounter lead him to the answers he so desperately sought? He leaned in, eager to hear the woman's tale, hoping that it would bring him one step closer to confronting Samuel Carrington and the evil that threatened to consume them all.

A DEADLY GAME

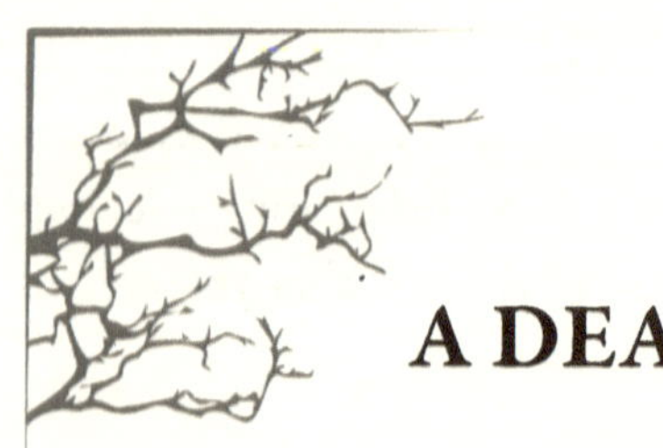

Ds Karl Cushnahan sat across from the mysterious woman in the dimly lit cafe, his curiosity piqued. Her words had hinted at a connection to the secrets of Ravenwood Manor, and he was eager to learn more.

The woman took a sip of her tea, her gaze steady as she began to speak.

"Detective, my name is Isabella, and I have lived in the vicinity of Ravenwood Manor for many years. I have seen the darkness that surrounds that place, and I know of the dark power that resides within."

Ds Cushnahan leaned forward, his interest growing.

"You know about Samuel Carrington and the mysteries of the manor?"

Isabella nodded solemnly.

"I do, but you must understand, Detective, that delving into those mysteries can be a perilous Endeavor. The forces at play are not to be underestimated. Samuel Carrington has tapped into a darkness that few can comprehend."

Ds Cushnahan's determination remained unwavering.

"I've seen the evidence of that darkness, and I won't rest until I uncover the truth. Can you help me?"

Isabella regarded him with a mixture of concern and caution.

"I can provide you with some answers, but you must tread carefully. Samuel Carrington is not an ordinary man, and his powers are formidable. He will stop at nothing to protect his secrets."

The detective nodded, acknowledging the warning.

"I understand the risks, but I can't allow his acts to go unchecked. What can you tell me?"

Isabella took a deep breath and began to share her knowledge of the history of Ravenwood Manor and the dark rituals that had taken place within its walls. She spoke of the artifacts that held ancient power and the spells that had been cast. She explained how Samuel Carrington had become entangled in a web of darkness, seeking ultimate power at any cost.

"As for the secrets of the hidden chamber," Isabella continued, "I can guide you there, but you must be prepared for what you might find. The malevolence within Ravenwood Manor is a deadly game, and you will become a player in it."

Ds Cushnahan listened intently, absorbing every detail. He knew that the path ahead would be fraught with danger, but he was willing to risk it all to uncover the truth and bring Samuel Carrington to justice.

Isabella looked at him with a mixture of sympathy and resolve.

"Detective, remember this—Samuel Carrington is a master manipulator, and his power knows no bounds. To confront him is to enter a deadly game, one where the stakes are higher than you can imagine."

Ds Cushnahan nodded, his determination unwavering. He had come too far to turn back now, and with Isabella's guidance, he would delve deeper into the mysteries of Ravenwood Manor, prepared to face the evil that awaited him.

As they left the cafe, the rain continued to fall, casting a shroud of darkness over their path. The battle between light and darkness had escalated, and Ds Karl Cushnahan was about to step into a deadly game where the line between truth and malevolence blurred, and the consequences of his actions would be dire.

Isabella led Ds Karl Cushnahan through the winding roads and dense woods that surrounded Ravenwood Manor. The rain had intensified, drenching them both as they trudged forward. The detective's heart raced with anticipation and a touch of apprehension, knowing that they were heading into the very heart of the darkness.

After what seemed like an eternity, they arrived at a concealed entrance to the manor—a small, ivy-covered door tucked away behind overgrown shrubs. Isabella produced an old iron key and inserted it into the lock, turning it with a creaking protest. The door swung open, revealing a narrow passageway leading deeper into the manor.

The air grew colder and heavier as they descended into the depths of Ravenwood Manor. Ds Cushnahan couldn't shake the feeling that they were being watched that the forces were aware of their presence.

Isabella's voice broke the silence.

"The hidden chamber is deep within the manor, Detective. It's a place where the darkest rituals were performed, where the artifacts held their power. But be warned—it is a place of malevolence, and you must stay vigilant."

As they continued their descent, the walls of the passageway seemed to close in, as if the very manor itself sought to keep them at bay. Ds Cushnahan's heart pounded in his chest, but he pressed forward, determined to confront the darkness head-on.

Finally, they reached a massive oak door, adorned with ornate carvings that seemed to writhe with energy. Isabella turned to Ds Cushnahan, her eyes filled with a mixture of determination and fear.

"Beyond this door lies the hidden chamber, Detective. It is a place where the power is at its strongest. Prepare yourself for what you may discover."

With a deep breath, Ds Cushnahan nodded, and Isabella placed her hand on the top right corner of the door. He heard a faint click and the door swung open. The sight that greeted them was both awe-inspiring and terrifying.

The hidden chamber was a vast, dimly lit space, its walls covered in intricate symbols and runes. At the centre of the chamber stood a raised platform, upon which rested the ancient artifacts—objects of unimaginable power.

As Ds Cushnahan approached the artifacts, he felt a palpable nastiness emanating from them. It was as if they held the very essence of darkness itself. He knew that this was the heart of the mystery, the source of Samuel Carrington's power.

Isabella watched him closely, her voice filled with caution.

"Detective, be careful. The artifacts are not to be underestimated. They hold the key to Samuel Carrington's power, but they can also be a weapon of great destruction."

As he examined the artifacts, Ds Cushnahan couldn't help but wonder what had transpired within these walls, what dark rituals had taken place, and how they were connected to Father Thomas's murder.

But as he delved deeper into the mysteries of Ravenwood Manor, he knew that he was only scratching the surface. The malevolence that lurked within these walls was a force to be reckoned with, and the battle between light and darkness had reached a pivotal moment.

Ds Karl Cushnahan was determined to unveil the truth, no matter the cost, and to confront Samuel Carrington and the power that threatened to consume them all.

As Ds Karl Cushnahan stood in the dimly lit chamber, his gaze fixed on the ancient artifacts that pulsed with evil energy, a realisation dawned upon him. The mysteries of Ravenwood Manor and the power of Samuel Carrington were intertwined in ways he had not dared to imagine.

Isabella watched him closely, her eyes filled with both concern and anticipation.

"Detective, these artifacts hold the key to Samuel Carrington's malevolence. But they are not to be trifled with lightly. They have the power to corrupt the soul and unleash unspeakable darkness."

Ds Cushnahan nodded, his determination unwavering. He had come this far in his quest for the truth, and he couldn't turn back now. He knew that confronting Samuel Carrington would be his only chance to end the reign of malevolence that had plagued Ravenwood Manor.

As he reached out to touch one of the artifacts, a surge of dark energy coursed through him. Visions of Samuel's acts flashed before his eyes—the car crash that had claimed his parents' lives, the night terrors and strange occurrences that had haunted him.

But amidst the darkness, Ds Cushnahan glimpsed a glimmer of hope—a way to break the hold that Samuel Carrington had over Ravenwood Manor. He turned to Isabella with newfound determination.

"We need to find evidence that ties Samuel directly to these artifacts," he declared. "If we can prove his connection, we can obtain a search warrant and put an end to his reign of terror."

Isabella nodded in agreement, her eyes reflecting a mixture of fear and resolve.

"But we must act quickly, Detective. Samuel is not one to be underestimated, and he will stop at nothing to protect his secrets."

Ds Cushnahan and Isabella left the hidden chamber, their hearts heavy with the knowledge of the malevolence that lurked within Ravenwood Manor. They knew that the battle between light and darkness had reached a critical point, and the stakes were higher than ever.

Back in the rain-soaked woods, they plotted their next move. Ds Cushnahan realised that he needed concrete evidence to tie Samuel to the artifacts and the power they held. But obtaining such evidence would not be easy, and the risk of confronting Samuel directly weighed heavily on his mind.

Isabella spoke, her voice tinged with caution.

"Detective, Samuel is a master manipulator, and he can sense our every move. We must tread carefully and gather the evidence discreetly.

There are others in the vicinity who may be able to help us, but we must be cautious in our pursuit."

Ds Cushnahan nodded, understanding the gravity of their situation. He knew that the path ahead would be treacherous, and that every move he made would be watched by the dark forces at play.

As they ventured deeper into the woods, the rain continued to fall, washing away any trace of their presence. The battle for Ravenwood Manor had become a dangerous pursuit, one where the line between truth and malevolence blurred, and the consequences of their actions could be deadly.

Ds Karl Cushnahan was determined to bring Samuel Carrington to justice, but he also knew that the sorcerer would stop at nothing to protect his secrets. The battle for Ravenwood Manor had reached a critical juncture, and the detective's resolve would be tested like never before.

THE SINISTER PLAN

As Ds Karl Cushnahan and Isabella ventured further into the woods, they knew that time was of the essence. Their quest to gather evidence against Samuel Carrington had taken a perilous turn, and the forces that surrounded Ravenwood Manor were ever watchful.

Isabella led the way, her knowledge of the woods guiding them to a hidden path known only to those who had lived in the vicinity for generations. She spoke of contacts—individuals who had encountered the darkness of Ravenwood Manor and might be willing to assist them in their pursuit of the truth.

With each step, Ds Cushnahan couldn't shake the feeling that their every move was being observed. He knew that Samuel Carrington possessed powers beyond comprehension, and the sorcerer's rage would be unleashed once he realised that they were closing in on his secrets.

Finally, they arrived at a secluded cabin nestled deep within the woods. Isabella knocked on the door, and it creaked open to reveal an elderly man with weathered features and a knowing glint in his eyes.

"Isabella," the man said in a hushed tone, "I sensed that you would come. What brings you here, and who is this detective?"

Isabella quickly explained their mission and the urgency of their situation. The man, known as Elias, had encountered the malevolence of Ravenwood Manor many years ago and had vowed to help those who sought to confront it.

"I can provide you with information and guidance," Elias offered, "but you must be cautious. Samuel Carrington's power is vast, and he will stop at nothing to protect the secrets of the manor."

Meanwhile, within the walls of Ravenwood Manor, Samuel Carrington had become aware of the intrusion into his domain. His rage knew no bounds as he realised that Ds Cushnahan and Isabella were closing in on his secrets.

His powers surged, causing the very foundations of the manor to tremble. Dark energy crackled in the air as he unleashed a wave of malevolence, sending objects crashing to the ground and shattering windows.

Samuel's eyes glowed with an unnatural light as he vowed to thwart their efforts. He knew that the battle for Ravenwood Manor had reached a critical point, and he would stop at nothing to protect his power and the secrets that lay hidden within.

As the rain continued to fall outside, Samuel Carrington's terrible rage reverberated through the manor, setting the stage for a showdown that would determine the fate of all those who dared to confront the darkness.

Inside Ravenwood Manor, Samuel Carrington's rage knew no bounds. He had become aware of Ds Karl Cushnahan's pursuit of the truth, and the detective's proximity to unravelling his dark secrets filled him with an intense fury.

In a chamber concealed deep within the manor, Samuel stood before a sinister altar adorned with the ancient artifacts. He knew that he had to strike back with a malevolence that would send a clear message—one that would force Ds Cushnahan to abandon his mission.

With a chilling grin, Samuel began to chant incantations, calling upon the forces that he had harnessed. Dark energy swirled around him, forming into ethereal tendrils that reached out, seeking his intended target.

Meanwhile, Ds Karl Cushnahan and Isabella were deep in discussion with Elias, gathering information about the malevolence that had plagued Ravenwood Manor for generations.

They were determined to bring Samuel Carrington to justice, no matter the cost. But as they delved deeper into their conversation, a sense of unease washed over them. Isabella's expression shifted, her eyes widening with dread. She felt a sudden, intense surge of malevolence—a psychic attack aimed directly at someone she cared deeply about.

Isabella clutched her chest, struggling to breathe.

"No," she whispered, her voice trembling. "Samuel... he's attacking my family. He's using them as pawns to force us to stop our pursuit."

Ds Cushnahan's heart sank as he realised the gravity of the situation. Samuel Carrington's retaliation had escalated to a new level, and the detective knew that he had to act swiftly to protect Isabella's family and continue his mission to uncover the truth.

With a sense of urgency, Ds Cushnahan, Isabella, and Elias rushed to Isabella's family home. The rain continued to fall relentlessly, adding to the ominous atmosphere that hung over Ravenwood Manor and its surroundings.

As they arrived at the house, the Carringtons and Isabella were greeted by a scene of utter chaos. Isabella's family members were gathered in the living room, their faces etched with fear and confusion. Some were pacing back and forth, their hands trembling with anxiety, while others huddled together in frightened whispers, casting wary glances at the dark corners of the room.

Isabella's mother, her eyes filled with tears, rushed forward to embrace her daughter.

"Isabella, thank goodness you're here," she cried, her voice trembling with emotion. "We don't know what to do. It's been like this for days—strange noises, objects moving on their own, and shadows lurking in the corners. We're terrified."

Isabella's father, his usually stoic expression twisted with worry, stepped forward to join them.

"We tried to explain it away at first," he said, his voice grave. "But then things started to escalate. We've seen things—horrifying things—that we can't explain. We fear we're being haunted by some malevolent force."

Isabella's siblings nodded in agreement, their faces pale with fear.

"It's been getting worse," one of them whispered, her voice barely above a whisper. "We can't sleep, we can't eat. It's like we're living in a nightmare."

As they listened to the harrowing accounts of Isabella's family, the Carringtons exchanged worried glances. It was clear that something sinister was at play, something beyond the realm of the natural world. And as they prepared to confront whatever dark force had taken hold of the house, they knew that they were facing a battle unlike any they had ever known before.

Samuel Carrington's power was wreaking havoc, and it was clear that he would stop at nothing to force them to abandon their mission.

Ds Cushnahan's resolve was unwavering. He knew that he had to confront Samuel Carrington, not only to protect Isabella's family but to bring an end to the malevolence that had plagued Ravenwood Manor for far too long.

The battle between light and darkness had reached a critical juncture, and the detective was determined to face the sorcerer head-on. But as they stood amidst the chaos, the stakes had never been higher, and the consequences of their actions would be dire.

As Ds Karl Cushnahan stood amidst the chaos wrought by Samuel Carrington's retaliation, he knew that the situation had reached a critical point. The safety of Isabella's family and the pursuit of the truth hung in the balance.

In the dimly lit living room, he turned to Isabella with a resolute expression.

"I have a plan, but it goes against my police values. It's drastic, but it might be the only way to confront Samuel Carrington."

Isabella, her face still filled with worry for her family, nodded in understanding.

"I'll support whatever it takes to stop him. What's your plan, Detective?"

After ensuring the safety of Isabella's family and stabilising the chaotic situation at her home, the trio regrouped with Isabella's contacts—individuals who had faced the malevolence of Ravenwood Manor and were willing to join the fight against Samuel Carrington.

In a hidden room illuminated only by flickering candles, they formed a circle, their faces etched with determination. Isabella's friends, each with their own unique knowledge of the supernatural, were ready to assist in the battle against the sorcerer.

Ds Cushnahan addressed the group, his voice filled with resolve.

"Samuel Carrington is a formidable adversary, but we have the element of surprise on our side. Together, we will uncover his secrets, weaken his hold on Ravenwood Manor, and bring him to justice."

The allies exchanged determined nods, knowing that their fight against the evil that had plagued Ravenwood Manor for generations would be a dangerous one.

As they plotted their next move, the rain outside intensified, casting a foreboding shadow over the landscape. The battle between light and darkness had reached a pivotal moment, and the consequences of their actions would be dire.

Within the walls of Ravenwood Manor, Samuel Carrington felt the weight of their defiance. His power surged in response to their gathering, and he knew that his reign of darkness was under threat.

In the midst of the rain-soaked night, the stage was set for a showdown that would determine the fate of all those who dared to confront the malevolence that lurked within Ravenwood Manor. The battle against Samuel Carrington had begun, and the skies themselves seemed to darken in anticipation of the coming storm.

THE FINAL CONFRONTATION

In the dimly lit room, Ds Karl Cushnahan, Isabella, and her allies huddled together, their faces illuminated by the flickering candles. The atmosphere was charged with tension as they planned their daring assault on Ravenwood Manor and the confrontation with Samuel Carrington.

Isabella's friends, each possessing unique knowledge of the supernatural, contributed their expertise to the plan. They knew that the power within the manor had to be weakened, and the artifacts responsible for Samuel's sorcery had to be destroyed.

Ds Cushnahan, his voice steady, outlined their strategy.

"Our first priority is to locate and neutralise the artifacts. They are the source of Samuel's power. Isabella, you and your friends will lead the way, guiding us to the hidden chamber."

Isabella nodded, her determination unwavering.

"Once we're inside the manor, we'll need to work quickly and stealthily. Samuel is a formidable adversary, and he'll sense our presence if we're not careful."

The allies discussed the intricacies of the plan, coordinating their movements and assigning specific roles. They knew that the battle ahead would be treacherous, but they were united by their determination to bring an end to the malevolence that had plagued Ravenwood Manor for generations.

With their plan in place, they ventured out into the rain-soaked night, making their way toward the looming silhouette of Ravenwood

Manor. The skies above seemed to mirror their anticipation, as if nature itself held its breath in anticipation of the final confrontation.

As they approached the manor's imposing gates, the group steeled themselves for what lay ahead. The battle against Samuel Carrington was about to reach its climax, and the fate of Ravenwood Manor hung in the balance. But there was a twist in the story, an unforeseen revelation that would test their resolve and change the course of their final confrontation.

Rain poured from the heavens, drenching Ds Karl Cushnahan, Isabella, and her allies as they made their way toward Ravenwood Manor. The path was treacherous, with muddy terrain and overgrown bushes, but their determination burned bright in the darkness.

Isabella led the way, her steps confident as she followed the hidden route she had known since childhood. Her friends, each with their unique talents, moved in silent synchrony, alert for any sign of danger.

As they approached the looming manor, the atmosphere grew heavy with foreboding. The forces that had protected Samuel Carrington's secrets for generations seemed to pulse with anticipation, aware of the impending confrontation.

They reached the manor's massive front doors, hidden in the shadows of the grand entrance. Isabella turned to the group, her voice a hushed whisper.

"This is where we go in. The hidden chamber is deep within the manor."

With their plan firmly in mind, they entered the manor, moving quietly through dimly lit corridors and winding staircases. The sense of malevolence grew more palpable with every step, as if the very walls of Ravenwood Manor were alive and watching.

Isabella's friends used their supernatural expertise to detect any wards or traps set by Samuel Carrington. Their caution was essential, for the sorcerer would undoubtedly be aware of their presence.

After what felt like an eternity of careful navigation through the twisting labyrinth of the manor, Isabella led them to a massive oak door. This was it—the entrance to the hidden chamber where the artifacts held their power.

Ds Cushnahan's heart raced as he realised that the final confrontation was within reach. They were about to confront Samuel Carrington and destroy the artifacts that had plagued Ravenwood Manor for generations.

Isabella pushed open the door, revealing the chamber beyond. It was a place where the power was at its strongest, where darkness pulsed with a life of its own. The ancient artifacts awaited, and the fate of Ravenwood Manor hung in the balance.

But as they stepped into the chamber, they were met with a revelation that would shatter their expectations and change the course of their final confrontation. The twist in the story was about to unfold, and the true nature of Samuel Carrington's malevolence would be revealed.

As Ds Karl Cushnahan, Isabella, and her allies entered the hidden chamber, they expected to find the ancient artifacts that had fuelled Samuel Carrington's power. Instead, they were met with a scene that defied their expectations.

The chamber was empty, devoid of any supernatural relics or artifacts. There were no sinister altars or energies. It was as if the source of Samuel's sorcery had vanished into thin air.

Isabella's friends exchanged bewildered glances, their expressions a mix of confusion and concern. Ds Cushnahan couldn't hide his astonishment.

"This can't be. The artifacts should be here."

Isabella stepped forward, her eyes scanning the chamber.

"I don't understand. This is where they've always been hidden. How could they disappear?"

As they searched the chamber for any sign of the missing artifacts, a sense of unease settled over the group. The forces that had surrounded Ravenwood Manor seemed to linger, as if mocking their futile efforts.

Just when hope seemed lost, Isabella's friend, Amelia, noticed a faint inscription on the chamber's wall. She approached it, her fingers tracing the ancient runes.

"There's something here—a message."

Isabella, Ds Cushnahan, and the others gathered around as Amelia deciphered the message. It revealed a shocking revelation that sent shivers down their spines—the artifacts had been moved, not by Samuel Carrington, but by a force far older and more sinister.

As the truth of the situation dawned upon them, the group realised that they were not the only ones seeking to confront the malevolence that had plagued Ravenwood Manor. Another force, one older and more cunning than Samuel Carrington, had played a role in the disappearance of the artifacts.

The revelation filled them with a sense of foreboding. They had entered a battle far greater and more complex than they had ever imagined, one that spanned generations and involved forces beyond their comprehension.

With the artifacts no longer within their reach, the group knew that they would have to navigate a twisted web of secrets and malevolence to uncover the truth. The final confrontation had taken an unexpected turn, and the battle against the darkness was far from over.

As they left the chamber, they realised that their mission to bring an end to the malevolence of Ravenwood Manor had just become even more perilous. The true nature had been unveiled, and the consequences of their pursuit were more uncertain than ever.

THE TWISTED END

With the revelation that the ancient artifacts had been moved by a force older and more sinister than Samuel Carrington, Ds Karl Cushnahan, Isabella, and her remaining allies were determined to track down their new location. The battle against the hostility of Ravenwood Manor had taken an unexpected turn, but their resolve remained unbroken.

Through careful investigation and a network of contacts, they had traced the artifacts to an abandoned crypt deep within the woods. The rain-soaked night was filled with tension as they approached their destination, knowing that Samuel Carrington awaited them.

The abandoned crypt stood before them, its ancient stone walls weathered by time. As they entered, the atmosphere inside was heavy with malignity. They knew they were walking into a confrontation that would determine the fate of Ravenwood Manor.

Their footsteps echoed in the darkness as they ventured deeper into the crypt. The artifacts pulsed with a sinister energy, their power growing stronger with each passing moment.

Samuel Carrington's presence hung in the air like a looming shadow. As they reached the heart of the crypt, Samuel Carrington emerged from the shadows, his eyes gleaming with malevolence. He had anticipated their arrival, and his powers were at their peak.

The battle that ensued was unlike anything they had imagined. Samuel's sorcery was relentless, and he picked off Isabella's friends one by one, each death more gruesome than the last. One of Isabella's friends, Julian, was ensnared by dark tendrils that constricted around him until he drew his final breath.

Another, Amelia, was subjected to nightmarish illusions that drove her to madness, causing her to take her own life. Isabella's childhood friend, Lucas, was consumed by a wave of darkness that left only a lifeless husk.

The last of their allies, Elias, attempted to confront Samuel head-on, but he was struck down by a torrent of energy. Ds Cushnahan watched in horror as his comrades fell, their deaths a testament to the twisted power of Samuel Carrington.

With each loss, their hope dwindled, and the malevolence of Ravenwood Manor seemed to grow stronger. Finally, it came down to a face-off between Ds Karl Cushnahan and Samuel Carrington. The crypt was filled with the eerie silence of impending doom as they circled each other, the artifacts' power crackling in the air.

As Samuel unleashed a torrent of spells, balls of flame shooting from his outstretched palms, Ds Cushnahan's instincts kicked in, his body moving with a fluid grace born of years of police training. He dodged and weaved through the onslaught, each movement calculated to evade the deadly magic hurtling towards him. Adrenaline surged through his veins, his senses heightened as he focused on the task at hand.

The air crackled with energy as spells collided with the ancient walls of Ravenwood Manor, sending sparks flying in all directions. Ds Cushnahan's heart pounded in his chest, the weight of their mission pressing down on him like a leaden cloak. But he refused to falter, drawing strength from the memory of his fallen comrades and the unwavering determination burning within him.

The battle raged on, each clash of light and darkness echoing through the halls of Ravenwood Manor. Samuel's powers surged with an intensity that threatened to overwhelm Ds Cushnahan, but the detective remained steadfast, his resolve unyielding in the face of adversity.

Despite the overwhelming odds stacked against him, Ds Cushnahan pressed on, his movements swift and precise as he danced around Samuel's attacks. With each passing moment, the battle grew more intense, the very air pulsating with the clash of opposing forces.

Samuel's eyes blazed with a fury as he poured all of his dark power into the fight, his every movement calculated to strike fear into the heart of his adversary. But Ds Cushnahan refused to be intimidated, his focus unwavering as he continued to evade each spell with the skill of a seasoned warrior.

As the battle reached its crescendo, Ds Cushnahan's determination burned brighter than ever, a beacon of hope in the darkness that threatened to consume them all. With every ounce of strength he possessed, he fought on, his mind clear and his resolve unshakeable.

The walls of Ravenwood Manor trembled with the force of their conflict, the ancient stones bearing witness to the struggle between light and darkness. But amidst the chaos and destruction, Ds Cushnahan remained steadfast, his eyes fixed firmly on his goal: to vanquish Samuel and put an end to his reign of terror once and for all.

With every spell dodged and every attack countered, Ds Cushnahan fought with a ferocity fueled by his unwavering dedication to the cause. He knew that the fate of not only the Carrington family but the entire world hung in the balance, and he would not rest until Samuel's reign of darkness was brought to an end.

As they fought, the crypt's ancient walls shook with the force of their confrontation. The fate of Ravenwood Manor hung in the balance, and the twisted end of their battle would determine whether light or darkness would prevail in the domain.

In the final moments of their battle, as spells collided and magic crackled through the air, Ds Cushnahan found himself facing Samuel with a determination that surpassed all fear. With a final burst of energy, he launched himself at his opponent, his movements fueled by the memory of his fallen comrades and the knowledge that he alone stood between Samuel and the darkness he sought to unleash upon the world.

As their clash reached its climax, Ds Cushnahan summoned every last ounce of strength within him, his resolve unwavering as he faced off against the embodiment of evil itself. And in that moment, with the fate of Ravenwood Manor hanging in the balance, he knew that he would stop at nothing to emerge victorious, no matter the cost.

The final showdown had begun, and the outcome remained uncertain as the forces of good and evil clashed in a crypt steeped in malevolence.

As the battle between Ds Karl Cushnahan and Samuel Carrington raged on in the depths of the crypt, the forces surrounding them intensified. Spells clashed, and the very air crackled with dark energy. It was a battle of wills, of determination, and of desperate hope.

Samuel Carrington's power ramped up, and he summoned his darkest powers to overpower his adversary. Dark tendrils of energy coiled around him, seeking to crush Cushnahan's resolve.

But Ds Cushnahan, fuelled by a deep sense of justice and the memory of his fallen comrades, fought back with all his strength. The crypt's ancient walls trembled as the two forces clashed, their struggle echoing in the darkness.

As the battle reached its zenith, Samuel Carrington unleashed a final, devastating surge of evil. The sheer force of his power overwhelmed Ds Cushnahan's defences, and he was unable to hold on.

Pressure suddenly increased in Karl's head, causing him to stop dead, clutching either sides, as if trying to prevent his head from splitting apart. His eyes were locked shut and nothing he could do would stop the pressure building. In that agonising moment, Karl's brain erupted under the immense pressure. He collapsed to the floor, lifeless, his eyes staring into eternity. Samuel Carrington stood over him, a triumphant smile playing on his lips.

With the defeat of his adversary, Samuel knew that he had triumphed, at least for now. The malevolence of Ravenwood Manor remained his to command, and the twisted end of their battle had claimed its final victim.

As Samuel Carrington looked down at the fallen detective, he knew that his power was unmatched. But there was one element he had not counted on—a force ancient and more powerful than any he had ever encountered.

The twisted end of their battle marked the beginning of a new chapter, one that would reveal the true nature of the evil that had plagued Ravenwood Manor for generations.

The battle between light and darkness was far from over, and the consequences of their actions would reverberate through the ages.

As the years passed, Samuel Carrington's power continued to grow, and he became a shadowy puppet master, exerting control over the world from the shadows. His ego knew no bounds, and he manipulated humanity in ways that were both subtle and devastating.

Samuel's influence extended to the highest echelons of power, where he manipulated world leaders and orchestrated conflicts that plunged nations into chaos. He sowed the seeds of discord and division, carefully ensuring that humanity remained oblivious to his true role in the unfolding tragedies.

Through carefully crafted schemes, Samuel pitted nations against each other, creating tensions that erupted into wars, all while concealing his hand in the chaos. He revelled in the suffering and turmoil that engulfed the world, all while remaining hidden from the prying eyes of those who sought to uncover the truth.

Under Samuel's influence, humanity descended into a state of moral decay. People turned against each other, their values eroded by the constant strife and conflict that seemed to permeate every corner of the globe. Greed, selfishness, and apathy became the norm as individuals looked out only for themselves.

The world Samuel had crafted was one where trust and compassion were rare commodities. The bonds of community and empathy had withered away, replaced by a pervasive sense of distrust and paranoia.

Samuel's reach knew no bounds, and he revelled in his newfound power. He amassed vast wealth, becoming the richest man in the world. He manipulated financial markets, controlled resources, and ensured that the world's wealth flowed into his coffers.

From the shadows, he watched as the world spiralled into chaos, convinced that he was the true master of it all. His laughter echoed through the corridors of power, a chilling reminder of the darkness that had enveloped the world.

"Look at the world around you," Samuel proclaimed to his unseen audience, "and tell me I am not succeeding." The world had become his playground, and he relished in the suffering and turmoil he had unleashed upon it.

But even as Samuel Carrington's power seemed unassailable, there were those who refused to succumb to the darkness. The battle between good and evil was far from over, and the hope of a brighter future still burned in the hearts of a few brave souls who dared to challenge the evil that had taken hold of the world.

DEAR READER, THANK you for reading my book.

I highly value your opinion! Please consider leaving a review. Your feedback helps other readers discover this book.

Thank You

Blake

Don't miss out!

Visit the website below and you can sign up to receive emails whenever Blake Patrick publishes a new book. There's no charge and no obligation.

https://books2read.com/r/B-A-DEZBB-UEWRC

BOOKS 2 READ

Connecting independent readers to independent writers.

Also by Blake Patrick

Chronicles of the Eternal Nile
Whispers of the Nile

Legions of Honour
The Eagle's Rise
The Briton Wars

The RIP Squad Chronicles
Pendle's Curse

Standalone
Fractured Shields
Hidden Cargo
Shadow of a Witch
Shadows and Solace
Whispered Promises
Predatory Waters
The Coin - Templar's Secret

The Castle On The Hill
Billy Witch

Watch for more at blake-patrick.co.uk.

www.ingramcontent.com/pod-product-compliance
Lightning Source LLC
Chambersburg PA
CBHW020724160726
47993CB00006B/2342